SKY PIRATES

THE DRAGON'S GOLD

D0348127

Praise for
SKY PIRATES:
ECHO QUICKTHORN AND THE GREAT BEYOND:

'Strap yourselves in for an exhilarating ride!'
Daily Mail

'Fizzes with magic and wonder'
Abi Elphinstone, author of *Sky Song*

'A charmingly madcap adventure'
Hana Tooke, author of *The Unadoptables*

'A tightly plotted, visual treat for the senses'
Nizrana Farook, author of *The Girl Who Stole an Elephant*

'A fast-moving adventure story'
Kirsty Applebaum, author of *The Middler*

'Pacey, thrilling and endearing too'
Joanna Nadin, author of the Rachel Riley series

'A breath-taking adventure'
Claire Fayers, author of *The Voyage to Magical North*

'An incredible adventure, brimming with friendship and danger'
The Bookseller

SKY PIRATES

THE DRAGON'S GOLD

ALEX ENGLISH

SIMON & SCHUSTER

First published in Great Britain in 2021 by Simon & Schuster UK Ltd

1 3 5 7 9 10 8 6 4 2

Simon & Schuster UK Ltd
1st Floor, 222 Gray's Inn Road
London WC1X 8HB

www.simonandschuster.co.uk
www.simonandschuster.com.au
www.simonandschuster.co.in

Simon & Schuster Australia, Sydney
Simon & Schuster India, New Delhi

A CIP catalogue record for this book
is available from the British Library.

PB ISBN 978-1-4711-9089-6
eBook ISBN 978-1-4711-9090-2
eAudio ISBN 978-1-3985-0000-6

Printed and bound by CPI Group (UK) Ltd, Croydon, CR0 4YY

For Ellie, Hannah and Jane

CHAPTER ONE

'I think I've found something!' Echo jabbed at the white sand with her shovel.

It felt like she'd been digging all morning in the blazing sun with nothing to show for it. Could this finally be the treasure they were searching for? Echo pushed her sweaty curls out of her eyes and crouched down to get a closer look. She had definitely hit something hard, but not solid like a stone. She turned her shovel over and scraped the sand away from the buried object to reveal the corner of something angular and brown.

'What do you think, Gilbert?' She stuck her head out of the hole to ask her little lizard, who was sunning himself on a nearby rock. He cocked a conical eye and then gave a tiny shrug of his golden-scaled shoulders before going back to sleep.

Echo glanced across the beach to where her mother, Lil, was digging. Lil's dark curls were wrapped in a spotted kerchief and she wore the high buckled boots of a sky pirate, although she'd taken off her plumed captain's hat and had left it lying on the sand.

'Mother ... I mean Captain!' Echo yelled. 'I think I've found something!'

'What is it?' Lil stuck the blade of her shovel into the sand and strode over.

'Look.' Echo pointed at the dark brown corner that stuck up out of the gritty sand. 'Do you think it could be the treasure?'

Lil squinted into the hole. 'Let me see.' She extended a tanned hand to Echo and helped her out, then hopped down lightly. She scraped at the corner with the toe of her boot, then squatted and brushed the sand away with her hand.

'Is it a treasure chest?' Echo was breathless with excitement. Had she really been the one to find it? The crew had been digging for hours and had almost given up hope, but Lil had insisted that they try one more time. And Echo's mother, Lil – Indigo Lil to most – had to be obeyed because she was the leader of the Black Sky Wolves, a crew of fearsome sky pirates, and captain of their airship, the *Scarlet Margaret*. Echo had grown up as a ward of the king of Lockfort, believing her parents had abandoned her on the castle steps. She had never stopped dreaming of discovering what happened to her mother though. And, when she finally did find her, she'd discovered that not only was Lil alive, but she was a famous sky-pirate captain. Echo still couldn't quite believe it was true.

Now that they were together, and Echo was the newest member of the Black Sky Wolves, she was determined to prove herself as a brilliant sky pirate too. It hadn't been easy so far though.

She held her breath in anticipation as Lil squatted down to examine whatever it was that Echo had found.

'I do think it might be,' Lil said, excitement rising in her voice. 'Fetch me my shovel, please.'

'Right away, Captain!' Echo flushed with pride. She jogged across to the hole that Lil had been digging beneath the star-palms and heaved on the wooden handle until the blade slipped free of the damp sand. She ran back, with some trouble as the shovel was so heavy, and passed it down to Lil.

Lil began scraping sand away with the edge of her spade and Echo leaned in to get a closer look.

Her mother stood upright and stuck her head out of the hole. 'Go and get the others. We'll need their help.'

Echo raced off, the sand hot beneath her bare feet and her whole body tingling with excitement. Please say she'd found the treasure! Ever since she'd seen the map that Lil had won in a grog-fuelled game of flip-the-frog at the tavern in Sleepy Palms, Echo had been determined to be the one to find it. It had been three whole months since she'd joined the Black Sky Wolves and, despite their many hunts for booty, she still hadn't seen a single real treasure chest. The haul of gold coins that was rumoured to be hidden in the salt caves of Tyger Island had proved to be a hoax. The legend of the Lake Lonesome diamond turned out to be just that. And even the Bonneville Hoard had slipped from their grasp when a rival clan of sky pirates, the Darkhearts, had beaten them to it, leaving only their signature heart-shaped token of black glass behind in the crypt.

In fact, from the strained conversations she'd overheard between her mother and Bulkhead recently, things were getting desperate. The *Scarlet Margaret*'s coffers were running low. But not for long! Not once she'd saved the day.

Echo pushed herself to run faster towards the other figures on the beach. Amberjack Bay was a skinny crescent of sand fringed with silvery star-palms. Their airship, the *Scarlet Margaret*, swayed gently in the air, tethered above the clear turquoise waters, its sails furled for the moment.

Up ahead, Echo saw the familiar profiles of the other Black Sky Wolves. Bulkhead, the *Scarlet Margaret*'s hulking first mate and chief navigator, was digging furiously. Slingshot, ship's lookout, was sipping water from a pigskin, his shock of white hair standing on end as usual. Beti, the gap-toothed ship's doctor, and Flora, the ship's boy, despite being a girl, dug in tandem, flinging sand rhythmically in opposite directions as they sang a bawdy sky shanty.

'Bulkhead, Slingshot!' Echo yelled, as she got closer. 'Flora! Beti! Come quick!'

The other sky pirates stopped digging and turned their heads.

'What's up?' Bulkhead looked up, his great bald head glistening with sweat.

'I've found ... something ...' Echo put her hands on her knees to get her breath back. 'Something large. I think it's a chest. Mother ... I mean Lil, I mean the captain is taking a look.'

The other four sky pirates downed tools and Bulkhead wiped his head with a purple handkerchief.

'At last!' Flora gave a huge grin as she hopped out of the hole she was digging and dusted the sand from her peg leg. 'I hope it *is* treasure this time and not another old boot.'

Heat rose to Echo's cheeks as she flushed, feeling silly for a moment. 'It's not a boot. Come and see!'

Bulkhead ruffled Echo's hair. 'Come on, mateys – let's see what Echo's got.'

It was all hands on deck when they got back to Lil. She scrambled out of the hole and swiftly set about issuing orders. Bulkhead and Slingshot were in charge of digging round the brown shape in the sand. Echo, Beti and Flora ferried buckets of water back and forth from the surf to soften the hard-packed grains. Lil stood and watched, a stern expression on her tanned face, her long, dark curls billowing in the breeze where they'd escaped from her kerchief.

Echo was grateful for the cool water on her bare feet and calves as she dunked her bucket into the foaming surf for the third time. She hurried back to the others.

'Watch out,' she said, and sloshed out the water as Bulkhead and Slingshot stood back. The sandy layer dissolved to reveal a dark brown oblong covered in rusted metal studs. A chest! Echo felt almost dizzy with pride.

'Will yer take a look at that,' said Slingshot.

'Aye,' said Bulkhead. 'She's only gone and found it.'

Flora crowded in next to Echo. 'She 'as as well.'

Real treasure! Echo couldn't stop the grin from spreading over her face as she took in the lid of the battered old chest. She'd saved their skins!

'We'll 'ave a feast tonight!' Flora turned to Echo and gave her a high five with one grubby hand, while Gilbert did a jubilant victory wiggle on Echo's shoulder.

'Stop that, you lot.' Lil's expression grew stern. 'There's no time for celebrating now. We're vulnerable until we've got this haul on to the ship.' She scanned the beach. 'Bulkhead, go and fetch the ropes. Slingshot, you two, back to the *Scarlet Margaret* and bring her closer.' She drew her cutlass. 'Bring Spud and Skillet down too. I'll stand guard.'

There was a murmur from the crew as they arranged themselves one behind the other along each rope. Echo positioned Gilbert securely across her shoulders and stood behind Bulkhead.

'Ready, Black Sky Wolves?' asked Lil.

Everyone grabbed the rope in both hands. 'Ready!' they all cheered.

'HEAVE!' yelled Bulkhead.

Echo braced her feet in the sand and pulled backwards with all her strength. In front of her, Bulkhead's broad back strained as, hand over hand, slowly but surely, they pulled.

'HEAVE!'

The rough rope burned Echo's hands. She almost stumbled backwards, but managed to stay upright.

'HEAVE!'

Echo could feel the coarse fibres tearing her skin. Her feet skidded and she landed on her bottom in the sand, but she kept hold of the rope, staggered back to her feet and gritted her teeth as she kept pulling.

'Nearly there!' yelled Lil. 'Beti – now!'

As the brown lid of the chest emerged from the hole, Beti leaped forward, the many bottles in her long skirts clinking, and grabbed its handles with both hands. The crew gave one final heave and, with a thud, the chest tumbled out of the hole and tipped on to the sand.

Everyone dropped the ropes, which rippled out on to the shoreline with a slap. Echo held her breath as Lil crouched down to brush sand away from the lock. What treasures would there be inside? Silver? Gold? Diamonds? Echo's mind spun with the possibilities.

'How're we gonna open it?' Flora's shrill voice cut through Echo's daydream.

Echo jumped up, putting her hand to the hairpin she always wore. 'I could pick the lock.'

'No need for that,' said Lil, brushing her aside. 'Stand clear, everyone.' She took a pace back and drew her musket from its holster, aimed and pulled the trigger. *BANG!* There was a crack of splintering wood as the chest disappeared in a cloud of gunpowder and smoke. When the air cleared, Echo saw that the lock had been blown clean off into the sand.

Lil wafted the last wisps of smoke away and strode forward. 'Bulkhead, a hand.'

Bulkhead positioned himself before the chest and turned to Echo. 'Come on – you too. It was you what found it after all.'

Echo grinned and raced forward to take her place between them.

'On my count,' said Lil. 'One, two, three, HEAVE!'

The wood was warped and so swollen with salt water that the lid was tightly wedged shut, but as they jiggled it Echo finally felt it loosening. With a *pop*, the hasps unfastened and the chest sprang open.

'Ready to see what you've found?' Bulkhead looked at Echo with a grin.

She nodded.

Gilbert's claws tightened on Echo's shoulder as she squinted into the musty darkness inside the chest. But she couldn't see anything. Where was the shining treasure?

Echo tipped the chest over and jumped back in alarm as a rather cross-looking octopus plopped out on to the sand.

It ... it couldn't be. The chest was empty.

There were disappointed cries from the rest of the crew, as everyone shuffled forward to see for themselves.

Echo stood apart, her arms folded across her chest. As she fought back the tears of disappointment that were threatening to spill, the octopus slip-slopped its way past them all and slid away into the water.

CHAPTER TWO

'Disappointing.' Lil kicked the chest with the toe of one battered brown boot and shook her head. 'Well, that's two weeks we've been searching Sleepy Palms and nothing to show for it. We're just going to have to give up and move on.'

Echo nodded, biting her lip to stop it from wobbling.

As they turned to go back to the ship, Bulkhead's kind brown eyes took in Echo's dejected face. 'Ah well, happens to the best pirates,' he said, ruffling her hair again. He squinted up at the sun. 'Nearly time to get your cousin from the aerodock,' he said. 'Wasn't he arriving at midday?'

Horace! Echo's disappointment dissolved into excitement at the thought of her best friend arriving. She'd been trying to persuade him to leave his studies and come to stay with her on the *Scarlet Margaret* for weeks until he'd finally agreed to pay a visit. At least *he* would be impressed by her tales of treasure hunting.

'See you!' she shouted over her shoulder to the others.

The town of Sleepy Palms was inland from Amberjack Bay, but to the inexperienced eye it was invisible as it was made entirely of tree houses hidden between the papery fronds of the trees. You heard it before you saw it, especially on market day. To get up or down, you needed to find a tree with footholds cut into the bark and climb up until your head popped through an opening and you could haul yourself up on to one of the rickety walkways that were strung between the palms.

Echo wandered over to the Sleepy Palms aerodock, a creaky platform of oiled boards where passenger airships landed. Gilbert nestled happily in the hip pocket of her breeches, with his head stuck out so he could snap at passing insects. Up ahead, Echo saw a small airship tethered in berth one and a scattering of people and suitcases waiting by the gangplank to board.

Echo checked Horace's message, received by postal pigeon – one of the little mechanical birds used to send notes to one another. Since her wolf's head hairpin had been stolen in the Violet Isles, Echo had recalibrated her pigeon to home to her mother's pin and now she could receive messages wherever the Black Sky Wolves went.

Arriving tomorrow on the noon Zeppelin from Port Tourbillon. The professor says hello. See you soon! Horace

Echo wandered up to the ticket booth, which was manned by a small ginger-furred monkey wearing a bottle-green peaked cap. As she approached, the monkey sprang beneath the desk with a screech, then reappeared holding a card marked: *Can I help you?*

'I'm meeting someone arriving on the midday from Port Tourbillon,' said Echo.

The monkey blinked for a moment, then ducked beneath the desk again and popped back up with another sign.

'Er, I think that's the wrong way up,' said Echo, tilting her head.

The monkey slapped its forehead and spun the sign round. It read: *Delayed*.

It then took a pair of binoculars from the desk and scanned the sky, before letting out an excited shriek. Extending one long, hairy arm, it pointed to berth three.

Echo turned to look behind her and saw, with a burst of exhilaration, the silhouette of a mid-sized passenger airship in the distance. 'Thanks!' she said, racing off to the berth to wait, all thoughts of her treasure-hunting disappointment momentarily forgotten.

As the airship neared, Gilbert let out a gleeful chirrup and Echo made out Horace's familiar blond head at one of the portholes. The ship descended, propellers whirring, to hover above the dock. As it came closer, Echo bounced up and down on her toes in anticipation. A crew of robots whizzed forward and lashed the airship's ropes to the mooring posts of the aerodock. Finally, the gangplank unrolled like a huge, metallic tongue and the passengers disembarked.

Sleepy Palms was the furthest outpost of the Eastern Airship line, hundreds of miles from the city of Lockfort where Echo and Horace had grown up, and even from Port Tourbillon, where Horace had been working as an apprentice to the famous explorer Professor Daggerwing. Only a few passengers descended from the ship. Echo soon saw Horace stagger down the gangplank, with a satchel slung over one shoulder, a little suitcase in one hand and a large book in the other. He looked rather green, Echo noticed, but he never had been very good at air travel.

'Horace!' she shouted, waving.

'Echo!' Horace smiled weakly as he approached. He dropped his suitcase on the ground in front of her. 'And Gilbert!' He tickled the little lizard under the chin and Gilbert's scales turned pink with pleasure. 'You both seem really well. The sky-pirate life must be good for you! You certainly look the part,' he said, taking in Echo's indigo velvet breeches and frilled cream shirt.

'Thanks!' Echo beamed with pride and her heart swelled so much the buttons almost popped off her jerkin. 'I don't have my cutlass or tricorne hat yet, but I will soon!'

'I suppose you have to earn them by doing something dangerous?'

Echo frowned, suddenly uncertain. How *did* she earn them? The other crew members all had a blade and a tricorne, even Flora, and she was younger than Echo. She shrugged, as if she didn't care at all. 'I'm not quite sure ... How's Lockfort anyway?' she asked, grabbing Horace's case. 'I hope your father isn't still making trouble?'

Horace's father, Alfons, had been the king of Lockfort, and for years had kept the outside world a secret from everyone who lived there. In fact, Echo and Horace had grown up believing there was nothing at all beyond the city walls. King Alfons had been trying to protect the people of Lockfort, but instead had made the city into a prison. In fact, if an explorer called Professor Daggerwing hadn't crashed his airship into Echo's bedroom window one moonlit night, they might never have learned the truth at all.

Echo shook her head as she thought how easily she could still have been stuck there, studying embroidery and deportment, and knowing nothing about Port Tourbillon or Sleepy Palms or the Violet Isles or anywhere else. The world had seemed so small back then. She thrust her hands into the pockets of her breeches. No, a life of freedom and adventure was the life for her. She was born to be a sky pirate!

'Father's still father,' said Horace, with a grimace. 'But he's stuck to his word and things are starting to change. The gates are open all the time now, and there's even an airship route from Lockfort to Port Tourbillon. To be honest, I haven't had to see too much of him since I've been in Port Tourbillon with the professor.'

After discovering the truth about the world outside Lockfort, Horace had jumped at the chance to leave and take up an apprenticeship with Professor Daggerwing.

'We're studying the evolution of the Lesser Spotted Stinkbeetle at the moment,' he said proudly. 'Would you like to see one?'

He reached into his satchel and Echo held her nose. 'Er, no thanks,' she said.

Horace continued to fill Echo in on all his latest research as they wandered back through Sleepy Palms, past the starfish market, the hammock shop and Persephone Pepperpot's Fine Hats for Fine Fellows, where Echo paused for a moment to peer in at the window full of jaunty tricornes.

Gilbert twitched his snout as the delicious scent of barbecued meat drifted by.

Horace's stomach rumbled loudly and Echo giggled. 'Feeling hungry?'

'Yes, rather,' said Horace, flushing pink. 'I was too sick to eat on the flight.'

'Let's get some lunch before we head back,' said Echo. 'Beatrix's crab dumplings are the best!'

She led him off down a bouncing wooden walkway in the direction of the smell. Soon they were feasting on crab dumplings, sweet-chilli noodles and a spicy peanut broth at Skitterbrook's Treetop Café – a cosy collection of sun-soaked bamboo tables, dressed with cheery pink tablecloths, nestled among the palm branches.

They ate in companionable silence, Echo pausing every now and again to offer a chilli noodle to Gilbert, whose scales flared bright red with every bite.

'This is delicious,' said Horace, leaning back in his chair and basking in the sunlight. 'I do love working with the professor, but I must admit it's nice to just relax sometimes. How long are we staying in Sleepy Palms?'

'Another two days,' said Echo, through a mouthful of dumpling. 'Then we're on to Trombones. There's rumoured to be a ruined temple in the jungle there—'

There was a sudden flash of blue and a brilliant turquoise-hued beetle landed on the table before them.

Horace put down his fork. 'How fascinating!' he said, his eyes sparkling. 'I do believe that's a Pearlman's Bl—'

With a snap, Gilbert sprang forward and devoured the little creature in one gulp.

'Well, it *was* a Pearlman's Bluenose,' said Horace, looking slightly shocked before breaking into a grin. 'I hope it was delicious.'

Gilbert bobbed his head as if to say, *Exquisite actually.*

Echo grinned back. She loved the sky-pirate life, but she had to admit it was good for the three of them to be together again.

After a dessert of creamy coconut-and-passion-flower ice cream, Echo and Horace meandered back through Sleepy Palms before descending from the treetop walkways to Amberjack Bay, where the *Scarlet Margaret* was moored.

Horace gazed up in wonder at the great floating airship swaying gently above the sand. 'I still can't believe this is your home!' he said. 'Doesn't it feel weird sleeping up there all the time?'

'Not really.' Echo shrugged nonchalantly, but secretly her heart swelled with pride. 'At first, I felt a bit airsick every now and then,' she admitted. 'But I guess I'm used to it now I'm a sky pirate.'

'It must be good to finally spend lots of time with your mother,' said Horace.

Echo shrugged. In truth, Lil had been so busy lately that Echo had barely seen her, let alone spent time with her. She brushed away the little wave of sadness that rolled over her and put on a smile. 'It's been great. Anyway, let's get your suitcase onboard.'

She shouted up to Flora, who leaned over the side of the ship and flung down a rope. Echo swiftly tied the end to Horace's luggage and gave a whistle to let Flora know to drag it up. The pair followed up the rope ladder.

Echo sprang over the side on to the deck. Horace came tumbling after her, landing face first with a clank.

'Ouch,' he said, retrieving a jar from his inside pocket. 'I forgot. Professor Daggerwing sent this for you.'

'How *is* the professor?' asked Echo, examining the strange jar. 'And the cats? And Mrs Milkweed? And what, exactly, is this?'

'Pickled ... er ... something,' said Horace, wrinkling his nose. 'I wouldn't eat it if I were you.'

They made their way down to the cabins and Horace unpacked his things.

'Come and see the crow's nest,' said Echo, hauling him back up to the deck.

'Are you sure?' said Horace, craning his neck to gaze up at the mast top. 'It looks very high.'

'It's perfectly safe,' said Echo. 'Just follow me. And don't look down.'

She sprang on to the rigging and pulled herself upwards, hand over hand, on the rough ropes. At first, she'd found it almost impossible to climb all the way to the crow's nest, but, as the weeks on the *Scarlet Margaret* had passed, it had become easier and easier. Now it seemed like the most natural thing in the world to be up there, the sea breeze blowing her hair, and breathing in salt brine and crisp, cool air.

She turned and looked down. Horace was still at the bottom of the rigging. 'Are you okay?' she shouted.

'Y . . . yes.' Horace took a wobbly step and clung to the ropes for dear life.

'Just take it slowly and keep going – the view's worth it!' Echo scrambled up the last few metres of rigging and heaved herself into the crow's nest. Gilbert sprang from her shoulder on to the wooden edge and peered down at Horace.

'Just a little bit further,' called Echo, as Horace grimly made his way, hand over hand, up to them. She pulled him in and he sat, panting, with his head between his knees.

'See, it wasn't so bad, was it?' Echo grinned.

Horace got his breath back and stood. 'Wow, what a view,' he said.

'There's the aerodock,' said Echo, pointing out the tiny landing strip where an airship hovered.

'And is that a volcano?' Horace waved at a squat

mountain in the distance.

'Mount Flameflux,' Echo said. 'We passed it on our way here. Almost singed our sails!'

Horace glanced down at the *Scarlet Margaret*'s sails, as if to check them for scorch marks, then he pointed down at Amberjack Bay.

'What are all those holes in the sand?' he asked.

'Oh, that's where we were digging for treasure,' said Echo.

'Treasure!' Horace's eyes widened as he goggled at her. 'Really and truly?'

'We didn't actually find anything.'

'But still – treasure hunting! You're a real sky pirate, Echo!'

'Not really.' Echo flushed with pleasure and stared at her boots. 'Come on,' she said, after a moment. 'We'd better get back on deck.'

But, as she climbed down the rigging, she couldn't help smiling to herself. She might not have a cutlass or a tricorne like Flora, but Horace was right: she was a real sky pirate, or certainly on her way to becoming one soon.

CHAPTER THREE

Echo and Horace clambered back down the rigging and jumped on to the deck of the *Scarlet Margaret*. They dodged Flora, who was busily sloshing soapy water across the wooden boards and mopping them vigorously, and wandered over to the stern of the ship, where Bulkhead could be seen in the captain's quarters, hunched over a chart with his sextant.

'How does the *Scarlet Margaret* float?' mused Horace, as he looked down at the beach below. 'I've always wondered. Professor Daggerwing's ship had a balloon filled with lifting gas, and an engine, and so did the ship I came in on from Port Tourbillon, but this one just has sails.'

Echo followed his gaze. Horace had a point. How *did* the ship float? The wind made them sail along, but what kept them up?

She frowned. 'I've never really thought about it.'

Gilbert squinted up at the sails himself and curled his tail into a question mark.

'You two look confused,' said Bulkhead as he emerged from the captain's quarters. 'Something got your tethers in a tangle?'

'Horace was just wondering,' said Echo, not wanting to admit that she didn't know either, 'how the ship floats.'

'Simple,' Bulkhead said. 'Cloud ballast.'

'Cloud ballast?' said Echo. 'What's that?'

'Ain't you ever wondered what all that rumbling is down below decks?'

'I . . . I thought it was the engines,' said Horace.

Bulkhead shook his head. 'Nope, we're all wind-powered.' He grinned. 'Come on, me hearties. Follow me and see for yerselves.'

Echo and Horace looked at each other and shrugged, then ran after Bulkhead, who had grabbed a bunch of keys from the captain's quarters and swung himself down the hatchway to below decks, his shiny brown head disappearing into the darkness.

Echo and Horace followed, clambering through the hatchway and along passage after passage. As they descended through the ship, the portholes grew smaller and the corridors darker. Echo passed her cabin and those of the rest of the crew, but they went even further down, past the galley, where Spud and Skillet, the kitchen boys, were stowing pans and sharpening knives, dancing round each other like two grubby white-clad ballerinas. Still deeper they went, to the very lowest level, where the barrels of food and grog were stored, past the locked copper door to the armoury, where weapons were stored and mended, and the infirmary where Beti stored her potions and tinctures.

In the three months she'd been aboard the *Scarlet Margaret*, Echo had explored every bit of the ship, or so she'd thought. Bulkhead opened a trapdoor she'd never noticed before and soon they were deeper in the belly of the *Scarlet Margaret* than she had ever been.

They were making their way through another gloomy, lamp-lit corridor when Bulkhead suddenly stopped.

Echo did too, and Horace bumped into her from behind.

'Ow!' They both yelped as they gave each other an electric shock.

'Wow, I've never even been—'

'Shh.' Bulkhead turned and put a large finger to his lips. 'Hear that?'

There was a rumbling in the boards beneath their feet, and Echo's hair crackled with static. Gilbert's tail stood on end.

Horace rubbed his arms nervously. 'I have a bad feeling about this.'

'What *is* that noise?' whispered Echo.

'That,' said Bulkhead, 'is the cloud ballast. Stand back.' He dropped to one knee and drew back the bolt on a final trapdoor in the floor. He cocked his head and tapped his ear as a rumbling sound came from below, rattling the floorboards beneath them. All the hairs stood up on Echo's arms and excitement fizzed through her.

Bulkhead pulled on the iron ring and flung open the hatch with a flourish. All three of them peered inside.

Beneath them, in the deepest recesses of the ship, the hold was filled with huge, writhing grey masses held in glittering nets. The grey things pulled and strained at the nets they were trapped in, as if trying to get free.

'What d'yer think?' asked Bulkhead, with a grin.

'What *are* those?' said Echo, leaning further in.

'Stand back,' said Bulkhead. 'You don't want to get singed.'

A sudden white zigzag of lightning fizzed across the chamber and lit Echo's and Horace's faces as they peered down. The air sizzled with electricity, and Echo breathed in the smell of ozone and burnt toast.

'But . . . but they're clouds,' said Horace, whose blond hair was now standing up on end. 'Wait, are they thunderclouds?'

'Exactly,' said Bulkhead.

'Thunderclouds?' That's what the rumbling was? Echo's mouth dropped open in astonishment.

'Yep.' Bulkhead put his hands on his hips and puffed out his chest proudly. 'Caught by yours truly.'

Echo could do nothing but stare as the clouds, dark as bruises, boiled and roiled in their nets.

As she watched, another shard of lightning shot from one end of the chamber to the other.

'It was Lil's invention,' said Bulkhead. 'Clouds float, see, so if you catch 'em, and stash 'em down 'ere, they make the ship float. No need for lifting gas, and the thunderclouds generate electricity too. With a bit more work on the generator, we'll be able to stop using coal altogether. Then there'll be no running out of power in the middle of a chase for the Black Sky Wolves.'

Echo felt her heart swell with pride. Her mother's invention! Lil was so clever to have thought of it. She glanced across at Horace to check his reaction, but he was frowning and still staring at the clouds.

'But where do you get them from?' he asked.

Bulkhead grinned, revealing a gleaming gold tooth. 'From the sky, of course.' He peered down into the hull at the clouds again. 'Tell yer what — some of these are looking a bit thin. Either of you fancy going cloud-catching?'

'How *do* you catch a cloud?' asked Echo, her head still spinning with a mixture of pride and sheer amazement at the thought that the ship was cloud-powered. An entire hold full of thunder under her feet the whole time, and her own mother's invention too! She shook herself and followed Horace and Bulkhead as they made their way back up through the airship's corridors and ladders, holding their noses as they passed the infirmary where Beti was now grinding up some rather pungent green roots with her pestle and mortar, and dodging Flora and her mop, which she was now sloshing vigorously round the corridors.

'And, if you need the clouds to make the ship float, how do you get up in the sky to catch them in the first place?' added Horace, as they emerged blinking into the sunshine.

'Ah, for that we use *Cloudcatcher*. She's stored up here,' said Bulkhead. He climbed up to the forecastle deck and opened a double-doored cabinet. 'Here she is.' With some effort and grunting, he dragged out a spindly metal contraption that looked like a two-seated bicycle with a horizontal propeller above.

'This is what we fly in and these –' he reached into the cabinet again and drew out a little bag – 'are the nets we use to catch the thunderclouds.'

He flung open the bag with a flourish.

Echo peered inside. It was empty.

Horace looked inside too. He turned to Echo and shrugged.

Finally, Gilbert scuttled down Echo's arm and inspected the bag, rolling his conical eyes around and curling his tail into a question mark.

Was this a joke? Echo looked at Bulkhead, baffled. 'There's nothing in there.'

'No?' said Bulkhead, with a grin. 'Look again.' He tilted the bag and, as the sunlight caught it, Echo saw something glimmer, a filament so fine and ghostlike it almost didn't exist. She blinked and it was gone again.

'Wait,' she said. 'I saw something. I did!'

Bulkhead grinned again. 'Try touching it,' he said.

Echo reached into the bag with one hand, scared of what she might find. Her fingers slid over a net of threads. It was like an unexpected cobweb brushing your face in the darkness. It was the sort of sensation that made all the hairs on the back of her neck stand up.

Horace reached in too, then looked up in wonder. 'What are they?' he asked.

'Aethernets,' said Bulkhead. 'They're woven by aether spiders from the Caves of Cape Cinnamo. Very rare, they are, but they're the only nets fine enough to catch a cloud.'

He lifted out one of the invisible nets, folded it and tucked it into his pocket.

'Right,' he said, 'I think we're ready to go. *Cloudcatcher*'s made for two, but if yer both squash in we three'll be fine.' He clapped his hands together and beamed at them. 'Who's ready to go cloud-catching?'

CHAPTER FOUR

Bulkhead squatted in front of *Cloudcatcher* and inserted a metal handle in a slot in the nose of the vehicle. He cranked it round once, twice, three times and the little engine spluttered into life. With a whirr, its propeller began to spin.

'Jump in!' he shouted above the roar.

Horace swallowed. 'Er . . . I think I might go and tidy my cabin. I don't want to leave my suitcase cluttering up the bunk.'

'Suitcases can wait!' Echo clambered into the passenger seat, pulling a reluctant Horace in after her. 'Look, there's even a seat belt.' She stretched the safety harness across them both and tucked Gilbert into the breast pocket of her jerkin, just his head peeping out.

Bulkhead passed the two children some goggles and pulled on his own before strapping himself into the other seat. He grabbed two metal handles in both massive hands.

'Ready?' he yelled above the whirr of the engines.

'Yes!' shouted back Echo.

'I suppose so,' whimpered Horace.

'What?' boomed Bulkhead.

'Yes!' Echo and Horace both shouted.

'Chocks away,' said Bulkhead, pulling back on the handles. *Cloudcatcher* wobbled up into the air, before soaring past the crow's nest of the *Scarlet Margaret*.

'*Oi!*' Slingshot, who was greasing the mast with an oily rag, ducked as they narrowly missed him.

'Sorry!' shouted Bulkhead.

Echo giggled and craned her neck to see Lil squinting up at them from the forecastle. Echo gave a cheery wave and Lil returned it, the creamy plume of her tricorne hat wafting in the breeze. Further below them, on the sand, she could make out the tiny figures of Spud and Skillet wading in the surf.

'Look!' She pointed them out to Horace. 'Maybe they're finding sea potatoes for supper.'

Horace took a quick glance down at the ground before grimacing and squeezing his eyes tightly shut. 'My favourite . . .'

Once they'd left the bay behind and *Cloudcatcher*'s motion had steadied, Horace finally dared to open them again.

'Where are we going?' Echo asked, as they whirred onwards.

'Mount Flameflux.' Bulkhead pointed one gloved finger at the horizon, where the volcano squatted, belching out plumes of smoke. Above it, Echo saw a purple-grey mass of clouds building.

'But ... but isn't that dangerous?' said Horace.

'Sky pirates ain't afraid of danger!' said Bulkhead. He steered the little vehicle out over the water, letting its nose drop into an alarming roll.

'But I'm not a sky pirate!' squeaked Horace, gripping the edge of the seat with both hands.

Echo grinned. 'Don't worry, you'll be safe with me,' she said.

As they approached Mount Flameflux, the storm crackled round them. Echo felt her hair stand on end with static. Horace squealed as a peal of thunder seemed to rumble right through Echo's bones, shaking the little flying machine and charging its frame with electricity. Gilbert ducked down in her pocket, putting both front feet over his eyes.

Bulkhead drew out the aethernet he'd taken from the bag and unrolled it on his lap with one hand while steering the little craft with the other. There was a huge crack of thunder and a bolt of lightning zigzagged down to the sea. The aethernet fizzed with electricity and Echo saw white sparks race along its fibres.

'Hold these,' said Bulkhead, swivelling the joysticks in Echo's direction.

Echo grabbed one in each hand, wrestling to control them as *Cloudcatcher* was buffeted on the air currents.

Bulkhead leaned out of his seat and whirled the aethernet round his head like a lasso, releasing a torrent of silver sparks that spiralled into the air. The net emitted a high-pitched whistling noise and the storm seemed to intensify, blowing *Cloudcatcher* here and there.

'Hang on,' said Bulkhead, as *Cloudcatcher* bucked and dropped, sending Echo's stomach into her mouth.

Horace let out a yelp that was lost in a great rumble of thunder. Lightning snapped round them, searing the sky with a blinding flash of white light that sent static crackling across Echo's scalp.

Bulkhead swirled the net one more time and let it go.

There was a flash as the net made contact with the cloud, but it slid off and the cloud seemed to roll away from them. Bulkhead reeled the net back in.

'Take her in closer,' he said.

Echo leaned forward over the controls, edging *Cloudcatcher* nearer to the eye of the storm. The closer the little vehicle got to the clouds, the harder it was to steer. Echo's very bones tingled as she grasped the controls.

Bulkhead threw the net for the second time. '*Aaaand* gotcha!' The net let out a dazzling spray of sparks as it snared the cloud, which bucked and writhed inside it like a wild animal.

Bulkhead pulled on the net, reeling it in.

Echo struggled to control *Cloudcatcher*, as the storm and the entangled cloud tossed them from side to side.

'Hold her steady!' shouted Bulkhead, as he fought with the net.

'I can't!' Echo grappled with the controls.

'I think I'm going to be sick,' moaned Horace.

Gilbert's scales turned a terrified white and he dived head first into Echo's jerkin pocket.

'*Gah!*' As the little vessel tipped on to her side, Bulkhead's hand slipped on the net and the cloud burst free, sending *Cloudcatcher* ricocheting backwards.

How stupid of her! Echo flushed with disappointment as she wrenched the controls down. *Cloudcatcher* spun through the air until, finally, Echo steadied their course and got them level again.

'Sorry,' she muttered.

'No worries,' said Bulkhead, panting. 'One more try and we'll have it.'

'Oh no,' groaned Horace. 'Can't we just go back?'

But his voice was lost in the wind as Echo glared at the boiling mass of clouds and steered *Cloudcatcher* back into the storm.

'Third time's a charm,' said Bulkhead, whirling the net round his head again. He let it go. There was a bang and a bright shower of sparks erupted from the aethernet as it sprang open and snared the cloud.

'Gotcha!' whooped Bulkhead, pulling back on the net with all his strength.

The cloud bucked and crackled, as if furious to be caught. Bulkhead wrestled with the net as *Cloudcatcher* was tossed about in the storm.

'Keep her level!' he shouted.

Echo fought against the juddering controls and tilted *Cloudcatcher* into the wind, where she could hold her steady against the violent breeze.

'That's it,' said Bulkhead, bracing his feet against *Cloudcatcher*'s metalwork and hauling the net in, hand over meaty hand.

The cloud tried to dodge this way and that, but it was well and truly snared. It hissed and fizzed, sending out showers of angry sparks, but it was no good.

Bulkhead deftly knotted the ends of the net round the writhing cloud, gave it a tug to make sure it was secure, and fastened it to one of *Cloudcatcher*'s struts. He slumped back in his seat and took back the controls.

Echo flexed her aching fingers. Her palms were slick with sweat and her curls were plastered to her forehead. She grinned in relief and glanced over at Bulkhead.

'Nice work,' he said. 'That is how we catch a cloud.'

Back on the *Scarlet Margaret*, Spud and Skillet had been busy in the galley, making a supper of crispy fried starfish, grilled squid tentacles and wedges of fresh watermelon. Once Bulkhead had stashed the fresh thundercloud in the hold, Lil and all the rest of the crew gathered round the makeshift table on the main deck, while Slingshot served out great spoonfuls on to their tin plates. Gilbert scuttled down to the table from Echo's shoulder and Slingshot tossed him a crispy tentacle.

'Told Horace about the treasure you dug up this morning?' asked Flora.

'You said you didn't find anything!' Horace turned to Echo, his eyes sparkling. 'What was it?'

The rest of the crew chuckled and Echo felt her face turn hot as she remembered the embarrassment of her discovery. 'Nothing,' she mumbled.

'Just one of those things,' said Bulkhead, nudging her kindly. 'Tuck in, girl.'

But Echo suddenly didn't feel like eating. She pushed her plate towards him. 'You have mine.'

'Oh, don't be melodramatic,' said Lil. 'Horace, Echo found a chest, but it was empty. It happens all the time. We'll find another, don't you worry.'

'I'm really not hungry,' Echo said. 'It's nothing to do with the treasure chest.'

'Nonsense.' Lil smeared her starfish with a spoonful of sea-tomato relish and took a greedy bite. 'Sky pirates need to keep their strength up. Who knows what might be round the corner? How did you find the cloud-catching, Horace?'

'It was ... eventful.'

'We did a'right in the end though, didn't we?' said Bulkhead, looking at Echo.

Echo flushed even redder as she remembered how she'd lost control of *Cloudcatcher* and the cloud had slipped out of the net. Being a sky pirate was harder than she'd thought. She took a quick glance at Lil, but her mother was absorbed in her meal and hadn't noticed Echo's red face. Echo sighed and nibbled at a wedge of watermelon.

'Come on, Echo, dig in,' said Slingshot through a mouthful of squid.

'Yeah,' said Flora. 'Are yer a pirate or a princess?'

A good-natured laugh rumbled round the table as they all grinned at her. Even Horace had a big smile on his face.

Echo lowered her gaze and stared sullenly at her plate, blinking away the tears that threatened to spill down her cheeks. More princess than pirate? She might have grown up in a castle, but she was one of them – a Black Sky Wolf! – wasn't she? A flicker of fear ran through her. Maybe they were only humouring her because she was Lil's daughter.

She scrubbed her eyes with her sleeve and after a few moments dared to look round the group. Nobody had noticed that she was upset. Horace was eagerly devouring his bowl of starfish. Bulkhead and Beti were laughing over a shared joke. Lil was leaning across the table to pour more grog into the grown-ups' tankards, her gold earrings glinting through her dark curls. Even Gilbert was too busy nibbling on a melon seed to notice how miserable Echo was. A wave of loneliness washed over her. Maybe none of them cared.

Flora caught her eye and grinned at her, and a flare of irritation lit in Echo's belly. She was no princess – she was a pirate. And she would prove it to them all, just as soon as she'd worked out how.

CHAPTER FIVE

The next morning, Echo woke to a chorus of birds and the chirrup of toads. She stretched, pushed off the covers and climbed out of her bunk, scooping up a sleepy Gilbert and curling him round her neck. It was early, five bells according to the ship's clock, and the airship was still very much full of sleep. The boards beneath her feet reverberated with soft snores from every direction.

As she got out of bed, Horace stirred in the hammock they'd made up for him in Echo's cabin.

'Where are you going?' he whispered.

'Up to see the sunrise. I do it every morning. Want to come?'

As they crept above decks, Echo peeped into her mother's quarters. Lil lay on her bunk under skull-and-crossbones blankets, one arm flung out above her head and the other clutching her cutlass. Her mane of dark curls had been tamed into a thick plait that hung down over the side of the bunk. She twitched but didn't wake. Echo smiled and crept up the stairs, followed by Horace. She eased open the bolts to the hatchway, pushed aside the trapdoor and shivered in delight at the rush of cool morning air.

Up on deck, the birdsong was even louder. Echo crossed the deck, careful not to slip on the fine mist of dew that glazed the boards underfoot. The sky was a pale lilac, just woken, and the palm trees rustled softly to themselves. Along the bay where they were moored, Echo could see that Sleepy Palms was still in darkness. Only the fisherfolk rose earlier than Echo, their airships tiny dots out on the horizon. It seemed everyone else in the world was still asleep.

'I love this time of the morning,' she whispered. 'It feels like it's all ours.'

'It's amazing,' said Horace.

Gilbert, who by now was clinging to her shoulder with one sleepy eye open, blinked, yawned and shut it again. Echo grinned. The day felt brimful of possibilities, wide open and untouched. She unrolled the ship's rope ladder and sent it unfurling down the hull, until the end landed on the sand below with a soft thud.

'Wait, what's that?' asked Horace.

Echo squinted as she peered in the direction he was pointing. Just above the palms, a tiny black dot was heading towards them. Echo shaded her eyes with her hand. From this distance, it looked like a postal pigeon. 'But who would be sending us a message here?' she said.

Horace's eyes sparkled. 'Perhaps it's an update from the professor on the stinkbeetles!'

'As long as it's just a message and not an actual stinkbeetle,' said Echo, wrinkling her nose. She ran to the gunwale and leaned out, ready to catch the bird. But, as it got closer, she realized it wasn't a postal pigeon at all. It was a mechanical bird all right, but much larger than a pigeon, with a long tail and a beak that was curved like a sickle. As the bird got closer, its metallic scales gleamed scarlet in the early-morning sun.

'I think it's a . . . a parrot,' said Echo.

'I do believe you're right,' said Horace, squinting. 'But a postal parrot? How peculiar!'

Echo staggered backwards as the bird hovered above the *Scarlet Margaret*'s navigation point, the metallic transmitter that allowed them to receive postal pigeons wherever they were. After a moment, its mechanical eyes whirred into focus as it zoomed in on first Horace, then Echo. There was a small beep and the bird swooped down towards Echo.

'Pieces of eight,' squawked the bird, as it landed on Echo's outstretched arm. She goggled at Horace. It talked!

The mechanical bird cocked its head at Echo and the eyes whirred again.

'Indigo Lil,' it squawked.

Echo stared in astonishment. She had thought postal

pigeons a marvel when she'd first seen one at the Mech Market in Port Tourbillon. The way you could dial in coordinates, write your message on a scroll of paper, put it in the pigeon's claw and send the little mechanical bird flying off to your chosen destination. But a talking parrot! This was a completely different machine.

'Message for Indigo Lil,' the bird squawked.

'But . . . but I'm not—'

'You are summoned to a meeting of the Seven Skies Alliance,' the bird carried on, ignoring Echo. 'The meeting is at the ice fortress on Shark's Fin Peak, midnight tonight. Transport will be provided from the drop-off point at Filigree Ridge. Come alone. No weapons. No exceptions.'

'But—'

'This message will self-destruct in five seconds. Please stand clear.'

The bird gave one last caw and swooped into the air, before exploding in a cloud of gunpowder and cogs.

Gilbert jerked awake, his scales paling in surprise. Horace ducked as a spring whizzed past his ear.

'But I'm not Indigo Lil!' said Echo in exasperation. 'And what is the Seven Skies Alliance?'

'We'd better wake your mother and give her the message,' said Horace. 'Can you remember what it said?'

'I think so.'

They raced back down the hatchway, Echo's mind

spinning with this strange new information. Postal parrots, ice fortresses, the Seven Skies Alliance! What could it all mean?

'But how can it have given *you* the message?' said Lil, when she'd been shaken out of her sleep and they had gathered with Bulkhead in the captain's quarters, with its flickering gas lamps and dark, wood-panelled walls.

'Is it because I'm wearing your hairpin?' asked Echo, touching the gold-and-emerald wolf pin she always wore.

'Postal parrots use facial recognition.' Lil frowned from where she sat behind her wide oak desk and drummed her fingers on a sky chart. 'Only sky pirates use them to communicate with one another.'

'Echo does look a lot like yer,' said Bulkhead. 'Them facial recognition valves ain't foolproof, yer know. Anyway, that's by the by. Who are we gonna send?'

Lil leaped to her feet and strode up and down the cabin. 'It has to be me.'

'But what if something happens—'

'I'm the captain. I'll go.'

'It could be a trap. Remember the time you were tricked by Madame Maja? Yer nearly ended up drowning in quicksand,' said Bulkhead.

'I got away, didn't I?'

'Only by the skin of yer teeth.' Bulkhead rubbed the back of his thick neck.

'Another reason that it should be me who goes.' Lil shook her head. 'What puzzles me is why the Seven Skies Alliance is meeting after all these years. What is Old Gus up to?'

'It's not him yer wanna watch out for, it's that Viper Voss,' said Bulkhead darkly.

'I can look after myself,' said Lil. She stabbed a finger at the chart. 'Filigree Ridge is only a couple of hours' flying time from here. You'll need to drop me there and collect me in the morning.'

'But who *is* Old Gus? And Viper Voss?' Echo asked. 'And what *is* the Seven Skies Alliance?'

Lil jerked her head up, as if she'd forgotten Echo and Horace were still there. 'Nothing to concern you two,' she said. 'Why don't you both go out and . . . swab the decks or something?'

Echo folded her arms. Swab the decks! Why wouldn't her mother let her in on these secrets? Was she a Black Sky Wolf or not?

'You never tell me anything!' she snapped.

'Echo, this doesn't need to concern you.'

'Because you think I'm more princess than pirate!'

'Of course not!' Lil's voice softened. 'But pirates follow their captain. You need to trust me on this.'

Echo sniffed and looked up at Bulkhead's kind face and Lil's unreadable one. Uncertainty squirmed inside her. Did Lil even want her here? Was Echo just a nuisance to her? She glanced at Lil's sword gleaming in her belt and tears threatened to build behind her eyes.

'What's wrong?' asked Lil.

'You don't think I'm a real pirate.' Echo forced her voice not to wobble. 'I don't even have a cutlass,' she mumbled. 'Flora does, and she's younger than me. It's not fair.'

'Flora earned hers, Echo,' said Lil sternly. Then her frown relaxed. 'But you're right. It is about time you learned to use a blade. I think we need to get you a cutlass of your own.'

CHAPTER SIX

Later that morning, when the sun was up and the monkeys were screeching in the coconut groves, Echo followed Lil through the wobbly treetop walkways of Sleepy Palms until they came to a part of town she'd never explored before.

Lil pushed the palm leaves aside to reveal a shop built of intertwined bamboo tubes.

'Captain Custard's Cutlass Emporium,' Lil said. 'The finest sky-pirate outfitter in all the Eastern Isles.'

Echo gasped, wishing Horace could see it too. She followed Lil inside and blinked as her eyes adjusted to the dim light. The walls were lined with shelves piled high with long, slim boxes. Nobody seemed to be in the shop, but Echo heard a metallic thrumming sound and voices that seemed to be coming from a back room.

Lil marched straight up to the counter and rang the bell. A moment later, a tall red-haired woman emerged. She pushed back her welding mask with calloused hands to reveal a pale face with a broad, freckled nose and shining green eyes. The woman grinned and thrust out a hand to shake Lil's. 'If it isn't Indigo Lil!'

'Good to see you, Concetta.' Lil slapped the woman heartily on the back.

'In need of a new scimitar to add to the collection? I've a fine Bonneville steel with a cherrywood grip. Or perhaps you'd like something more traditional?'

Concetta ducked under the counter and emerged with a long box. She blew the dust off, making Lil blink, Echo sneeze and Gilbert scuttle down the neck of Echo's shirt.

'This,' the woman went on as she opened the box with a flourish, 'is an antique scimitar handcrafted by the goldsmiths of Pomegranth.' She took out a curved sword so sharp it almost disappeared when she turned it in the light. 'Here, try it.' She offered the hilt to Lil.

Lil shook her head. 'I'm not here for a sword for myself,' she said, although Echo noticed she cast a longing glance at the blade. Lil licked her lips. 'Although I suppose it wouldn't hurt just to try it.'

'Precisely.' Concetta grinned, revealing one diamond-studded incisor. 'Put her through her paces.'

Lil gave the scimitar an experimental swing, cutting the blade through the air with a *swish*. 'So light,' she said admiringly.

'And only ninety doubloons.'

Lil nodded slowly. 'Thank you, but no,' she said, carefully

handing the scimitar back. 'I'm here to buy a first sword for my daughter.'

Echo stood up a little straighter, her eyes still fixed on the shining scimitar.

'Your ... Oh!' Concetta looked at Echo, as if suddenly noticing her. 'A first sword. What an honour! Let's get you measured up then. I'm sure I have just the thing for you.'

She scurried back behind the counter and returned with a battered brown leather suitcase, which she placed on the floor at Echo's feet, before flicking open the brass clasps and opening it out. Inside, one half of the case was covered in dials and switches, while the other was empty and lined with soft brown velvet. There were two indents in the velvety surface like bootprints in mud.

'Please step in,' the red-haired woman said.

Echo stared at the case. What in the seven skies was the woman going to do to her? She only wanted a cutlass. She swallowed and looked at Lil. 'In there?' she said, pointing at the indents.

'Go on,' said Lil. 'I'm sure it's quite safe. Concetta Custard's been fitting sky pirates with their first cutlasses since before you were born. Although I have to admit,' she said, 'I haven't seen this particular method before.'

'Oh yes, it's the latest technology. The Bivalve Aether-powered Fit-o-Matic 6000. Selects the perfect blade every time,' said Concetta.

Echo stepped into the foot-shaped indents and waited nervously while Concetta fiddled with the knobs and dials in the lid of the contraption. There was a whirring sound and Echo jumped as she felt the footbeds close gently round her feet, as if they were being gently squeezed by two giant hands. With a creak, something sprang out of the case behind her back and extended towards the ceiling. She looked up to find a huge brass claw opening above her.

'Stand perfectly still,' said Concetta. 'Just taking a few measurements.'

The claw opened and encircled Echo's head with its splayed prongs, before gently grasping her skull. There was some more whirring. The red-haired woman muttered under her breath as she continued to flip switches and frown at the meter.

'Stretch both arms out to the side,' she said. 'Like this.' She spread both arms out like wings.

Echo copied and couldn't help giggling as the claw released her head and disappeared behind her. Now, two long brass arms popped out of a slot somewhere near the toes of her boots. They extended until they encircled her wrists. Then the machine bleeped, the arms slid back into the case with a clunk and Echo felt the footholds release their grip on her boots. There was a humming noise that vibrated right through the soles of her feet and a reel of printed paper came rattling out of an opening in the machine.

Concetta pulled it free and put her glasses on to her nose to examine it.

'Can I get out now?' said Echo, eager to be free of the case.

'Yes ... yes ...' Concetta absent-mindedly waved her away, still absorbed in the printout from the Fit-o-Matic.

'What does it say?' asked Echo. What sort of sword would the machine have chosen for her? A vicious cutlass with a wolf-engraved hilt like Lil's? Or maybe a smaller but no less deadly gleaming steel blade like Flora's. Or perhaps even a chunky, yet razor-sharp machete, like the one Bulkhead sometimes carried in his belt.

'Interesting,' said Concetta. A smile broke out on her face and she looked at Echo with new enthusiasm. 'An interesting prescription for an interesting sky pirate! It seems a lava-forged rapier is in order!'

'A rapier?' said Lil, frowning. 'But that's not much of a pirate sword.'

'The Fit-o-Matic says it quite clearly.' Concetta waved the printout at Lil.

'Couldn't you just measure her up in the usual fashion?' Echo could hear the disappointment in Lil's voice and her own stomach swirled.

Concetta shook her head. 'Afraid not. The Fit-o-Matic is always right and I have just the thing. Now, where is it ... ?'

She took out a small, copper-riveted stepladder and cranked a handle on it until it extended upwards with a small *hiss* of steam. She climbed to the very top shelf, revealing buttoned black boots beneath her many layers of petticoats. After rooting around on the shelf, she finally found what she was looking for and returned with one of the long, slim boxes. It was disintegrating with age and covered in cobwebs.

Gilbert emerged from Echo's collar and cocked an inquisitive eye as Concetta opened the box, sending a family of spiders scurrying across the counter. She pulled out a short, straight sword about the length of Echo's forearm and unsheathed it from its scabbard. It was a dull grey, skinny and perfectly straight with a pointed tip.

Echo looked at the little mottled blade and her stomach grew heavy with disappointment. Even the Fit-o-Matic seemed to know she wasn't much of a sky pirate.

'Want to try her?' Concetta said.

Echo swallowed and nodded. 'Thank you,' she said, taking the hilt in her hand. The little sword was light and comfortable in her grip, despite its small size, and, to Echo's surprise, it seemed to fit her hand perfectly. She waved the blade like Lil had, feeling silly as she didn't know what to do, but the sword gave a pleasing *zing* as it cut through the air. Maybe this was the right sword for her after all?

She smiled at Lil. 'It doesn't look like your cutlass.'

'That's because it's not a cutlass,' said Lil, taking the sword and examining it. 'It's a rapier. But it's probably safer for a beginner.'

'Her name's *Stinger*,' said Concetta. 'Crafted by the famed swordsmiths of the Scrimshaw Volcano forges. And only seventy doubloons.' She grinned. 'What do you say?'

Lil put *Stinger* back on the counter.

Echo held her breath. 'Mother?'

Lil looked into her drawstring pouch and frowned. 'I suppose there's no chance of a discount. For old times' sake?' she asked.

'Afraid not,' said Concetta, with a firm smile.

Lil emptied the contents of her purse on to the counter and counted out the last of the gold coins into seven neat piles. 'Seventy doubloons it is.'

Concetta sheathed the little sword and handed it to Echo. 'Take good care of her and she'll take good care of you.'

'I will,' said Echo, feeling the weight of the blade in her hands.

Gilbert scuttled down her arm and flicked out his tongue, then cocked his head at Echo in a way that said, *Impressive*.

'Come on,' said Lil, tipping her hat at Concetta. 'Let's get back to the ship. I think you're in need of some fighting lessons.'

Echo hugged *Stinger* to her chest and followed Lil out, unable to stop herself from smiling. It might not be a cutlass, but it was still her very own sword. Perhaps she was a real sky pirate after all.

CHAPTER SEVEN

Echo followed Lil down the cramped corridors of the *Scarlet Margaret* to the armoury. Lil had allowed Horace to come too and, although he hadn't really wanted to (being somewhat allergic to fighting lessons), Echo's pleading had finally persuaded him to tear himself away from the beetle books he'd been reading and join her.

They stopped at the end of a dimly lit corridor. Lil took a large key out of her pocket and unlocked the copper-clad door.

'Welcome to the armoury,' she said. 'Flora will take things from here.'

'Flora?' Echo frowned in confusion and turned to see the younger girl had appeared behind them. 'But I thought you were teaching us to fight?'

'I'm afraid not. I have my captain's duties to attend to. We need to sell off some of the emergency booty. There's no gold left in the coffers and we have to buy supplies before we leave for Trombones.'

'But . . . but she's not even a grown-up!' Echo scowled.

'Flora is known for her fast footwork and excellent swordsmanship,' said Lil. She turned to Flora. 'Make sure they work hard.' Lil patted Echo brusquely on the shoulder and marched back up the corridor, the key still swinging from her fingers.

Echo gazed after her, squashing down the disappointment so that Flora didn't see. She'd barely spent any time with Lil for weeks. And how could Flora teach her anything? Echo was older than her! She folded her arms and glared at the younger girl's back as she swung the door open in front of them.

'Coming?' Flora looked round quizzically at Echo.

'Of course.' Echo forced a smile on to her face. She would just have to get this lesson over and done with and find an opportunity to show Lil her skills later.

Inside, the armoury was so gloomy Echo that could barely make anything out.

'Shall I fetch a lamp?' asked Horace.

'No!' Flora snapped. 'No naked flames in the armoury. There's so much gunpowder in here the whole airship might go up!' She took down a jar that was hanging from a hook on the wall and gave it a shake. Immediately, it lit up with an eerie greenish glow. 'In the armoury, we use glowbugs.'

'Glowbugs?' Horace stepped forward, all feelings of

trepidation forgotten. 'Are they really . . .' He peered into the jar. 'Why, yes, they are! How fascinating!'

Gilbert emerged from Echo's pocket and leaped on to the wall, climbing with his sticky toes until he reached the jar. He butted it gently with his snout and stared at the little bug crawling around inside.

'They're not for eating.' Flora grinned. 'Why don't you two wake the rest of 'em up while I get the cutlasses ready?'

Echo and Horace circled the room, gently shaking the jars and waking the little creatures, until the whole room was filled with light. Now Echo could see rows and rows of cutlasses gleaming on one wall, an array of flintlock pistols on another and, in one corner, a huge rack of cannonballs. Barrels of gunpowder were stacked to the rafters in another corner.

Echo hugged herself with excitement. She was going to be a real sky pirate! A fighter! 'Just look at all these weapons!' she whispered to Horace.

Horace swallowed. 'They look sharp.'

'They *are* sharp,' said Flora. 'Sharpest set of cutlasses in all the seven skies.'

The seven skies. Echo suddenly thought back to the postal parrot's message about the Seven Skies Alliance. She cleared her throat and leaned casually on a barrel. 'Do you know anything about the Seven Skies Alliance, Flora?' she asked.

'Never 'eard of it,' said Flora, opening a large wooden chest. 'All I know is there are seven sky-pirate clans – us, the Scurvy Sea Snakes, the Darkhearts, the Pitiless Plunderers, the Heartless Violet Pilots, the Stormshakers and the Thunder Sharks, of course. They're the absolute worst!'

'Why?' Echo's eyes grew wide.

Flora's voice dropped to a whisper. 'They say their leader, Old Gus, keeps a shark tank in the hold of their ship. And if someone crosses him . . . he feeds 'em to the sharks!'

Horace gulped loudly.

Gilbert's scales turned white and he hid his face in the collar of Echo's shirt.

'Anyway, both of yer take one of these,' Flora said brightly, reaching into the chest. She held out two blunt, stubby swords made of a waxy yellowish wood.

'Thanks.' Horace stepped forward and took his.

But Echo couldn't stop the feeling of disappointment that flooded through her. These were children's swords! Was Flora mocking her again?

'Why can't I use *Stinger*?' she asked.

Flora grinned gappily. 'Master these, then yer'll be ready for *Stinger*.'

'But they're for babies!'

'They're for novices. Everyone has to start somewhere.' Flora held out the wooden sword. 'Here.'

Echo frowned and took it. Did Flora think she couldn't handle a real cutlass? She felt her cheeks flush with shame. Did Lil? As Flora turned away to open another chest, Echo swiped the sword clumsily through the air and winced at the disappointingly un-swishy sound it made.

Horace turned to her. 'Well, I'm glad we're only using practice blades. I was worried she was going to make us fight with real ones!'

Echo scowled in response and turned to see Flora wheeling over a strange, headless robot with two blunt swords for arms. Great, so they weren't even going to be fighting a real person.

'Meet yer swordsmanship tutor, the Swashbucklatron,' Flora said. She pressed a button on the robot's shoulder and, with a clank, it began to jab and parry blows at them.

Horace leaped back, clutching his sword to his chest in terror.

Echo made a running attack, but the Swashbucklatron blocked her blow and she tumbled to the floor, landing awkwardly on one elbow.

'Not so fast, Echo.' Flora chuckled and Echo flushed in annoyance.

Flora hauled her to her feet. 'Let me demonstrate first.' She took a cutlass with a golden hilt encrusted with emeralds from the wall and turned to face the robot. The Swashbucklatron swished its blades and Flora retreated for a moment, then darted forward and, with a quick wrist-flick, disarmed it of both its swords. They clattered to the floor and the robot gave a dismal bleep.

Echo narrowed her eyes. Flora must be cheating somehow. How had she managed that?

'It's all about knowing when to attack and when to retreat,' said Flora brightly, replacing the cutlass in its rack. She scooped up the robot's blades and reattached them. 'Have another go.'

'Fine.' Echo faced the Swashbucklatron again, imagining it was Flora she was about to attack. But, however hard she tried, Echo couldn't disarm even one of the robot's blades. It was hot work and, by the time the lesson was finished, her shirt was soaked through with sweat, her palm was sore and blistered and her cheeks were scarlet with irritation.

'Good effort, both of yer,' said Flora, when they'd finally finished.

'Thanks,' said Horace, wiping the sweat from his forehead. 'It's much harder than it looks, right, Echo?'

Echo nodded, too cross and tired to speak. She needed to practise, but by herself, without Flora sniggering at her. She wiped her hands on her breeches. 'When's our next lesson?' she asked. As much as she'd hated the Swashbucklatron, she needed to master the wooden sword so Lil would let her have *Stinger*.

'I have a new task for yer before you're ready for yer next lesson,' said Flora. 'Down on the beach.'

Horace looked nervously at Echo. 'We're not going to have to fight each other, are we?'

'No fighting,' said Flora. 'This is an exercise in stealth. Have you ever noticed those little blue crabs?'

'Yes,' said Echo, wrinkling her brow in confusion. What did crabs have to do with sword fighting?

'I've seen them too,' said Horace. 'I wanted to get a closer look, but when we walked past they all scuttled into their holes and hid.'

'Exactly,' Flora said. 'Those crabs are always on the alert. They're observant. It's almost impossible to sneak up on 'em.' She looked at them. 'Almost but not completely.'

'But I don't see what this has got to do with learning to use my sword,' said Echo.

'If yer can tap three crabs on the top of their shell with the tip of yer blade, then you're ready for yer next lesson,' said Flora. 'You too, Horace.'

'But . . .' said Echo. 'That's ridiculous! This isn't going to teach me anything at all!'

'So you're saying you can already do it?' Flora raised one eyebrow.

Echo swallowed. 'No.'

'Off yer go then.' Flora turned away to wheel the Swashbucklatron back to its storage chest, leaving Echo staring, open-mouthed and furious, the silly wooden sword still clutched in one hand.

CHAPTER EIGHT

Echo's mood hadn't improved by the time they returned from the beach.

'What's the matter, Echo?' asked Horace, taking in her sullen face as she stomped below decks after supper. 'Crab-catching was fun!'

'I don't want to have fun,' snapped Echo. 'I want to learn to be a sky pirate. A *proper* sky pirate. And I don't see how messing about with crustaceans is going to help me.'

'Flora knows what she's doing,' said Horace. 'Maybe she has her reasons.'

'Or maybe she's just trying to make me look like a fool,' said Echo. 'I swear those crabs were laughing at us.' She sighed. She really needed to talk to Lil about the lessons. Maybe if she explained the ridiculous task Flora had set them, her mother would agree to teach them herself? But Lil had been holed away in the captain's quarters, too busy with 'important 'matters' to be disturbed. She hadn't even joined the rest of the crew for supper.

As they passed Lil's cabin, Gilbert gave a soft chirrup and cocked his head.

'What is it?' Echo stopped to listen. Hushed voices were coming from Lil's cabin. Echo signalled to Horace to be quiet, crept forward and put her ear to the door.

'It's too dangerous.' It was a man's voice – Bulkhead's, Echo realized.

Lil replied in an irritated whisper. 'I have no choice. I can't ignore it.'

'Then let me come with yer.'

'It's against the rules of the alliance.'

'Well, I think we should at least tell the rest of the crew—'

'Absolutely not. I'll get this over and done with – nobody needs to know.'

'But, Lil—'

'That's Captain to you.'

'Yes, Cap'n.' Echo heard Bulkhead sigh. 'I'm worried, that's all.'

'That'll be all, First Mate.' Lil's voice was stern.

Echo slunk back into the shadows just as the door burst open and Bulkhead stormed out, slamming it behind him without looking round.

She waited for him to disappear down the corridor before beckoning Horace to follow her into their cabin. She eased the door closed and sat down on her bunk.

'What was all that about?' Horace said.

'I'm not quite sure, but something's going on,' said Echo. She frowned. Lil had mentioned the alliance. The postal parrot suddenly popped into her mind again. The Seven Skies Alliance. Was that what Lil and Bulkhead had been arguing about? Echo's skin froze. Was Lil planning something dangerous?

'You look worried,' said Horace. 'Please tell me what's happening. Are we in danger?'

Echo shook her head. 'Not us – Lil.'

'Phew,' Horace breathed.

'Thanks for being so caring,' snapped Echo.

'I just mean ... Lil's used to danger. She's a sky-pirate captain! I'm sure she'll know what to do.'

'I guess.' Echo wrapped her arms round herself. Horace was right – Lil was an experienced sky pirate. She wouldn't be so silly as to put herself in danger. But something about Lil's tone of voice niggled at Echo. She knew how it felt to pretend to be brave, and that's just how Lil had sounded.

Late that night, Echo woke in darkness to find her hammock rocking gently with the movement of the ship. Strange – were they travelling by night? Confused, she leaned over and lifted the edge of the porthole cover. They *were* moving, and down below the ship, where she'd expected to see the curved bay and gently swishing star-palms, were jutting mountains tipped with snow. The Black Sky Wolves never travelled by night unless they had to, and they weren't supposed to be leaving Sleepy Palms for two more days. What was happening? Echo frowned. Then her heart clenched as she remembered Lil and Bulkhead's hushed argument. Lil *was* going to the meeting with the Seven Skies Alliance. She had to be!

Echo flung her covers back and pulled on her socks and breeches, buttoned up her shirt and fastened her jerkin. She trod softly to the door, only pausing to grab her boots and knapsack, pin her mother's wolf's head hairpin on to her curls for luck and scoop a sleepy Gilbert on to her shoulder. She inched the door open and flinched as it gave a soft *creeeeak*.

There was a rustle behind her and Echo spun round.

'Echo.' Horace sat up in his hammock and blearily rubbed his eyes. 'What are you doing?' he mumbled.

'The ship's moving. I'm going up to see what's happening.'

The *Scarlet Margaret* lurched forward in a sudden burst of speed, sending Horace's spyglass rolling across the floor. 'Wait, I'm coming too.' He flung his legs out of his hammock and hopped down, before shoving the spyglass into his satchel.

'Sure?'

'Well, I don't want to be here on my own if something's happening.' Horace tugged on his jerkin and hopped to pull on his boots.

'Quietly then, and don't be a pudding heart.'

'I won't!'

Echo crept out of the door and down the dimly lit passageway, trying to avoid the creakiest boards. When she reached the top of the stairs to the main deck, she found the bolt to the hatch already drawn. She cautiously pushed up the trapdoor and peeked out.

In the moonlight, she could see Bulkhead in the wheelhouse, steering the ship with his back to them. At the rear of the deck, Lil stood with a coil of mooring rope, ready to fling it over the side.

Echo eased the hatch completely open and crept out, with Horace close behind her.

They slipped behind some barrels and Echo's stomach lurched as Bulkhead guided the airship down. This must be Filigree Ridge, the drop-off point in the postal parrot's message. After a few moments, Lil threw the coil of rope. There was a muffled shout from below and the boards beneath them tilted as the rope tightened on its mooring. Lil gave a brief salute to Bulkhead, then hopped neatly over the side and disappeared down the rope ladder.

Echo swallowed, her throat suddenly thick with fear. Just like that, Lil was gone. What if Bulkhead had been right and it was a trap? Lil hadn't even said goodbye.

Bulkhead smoothly wheeled the *Scarlet Margaret* round and set her on a course away from Filigree Ridge. Down below, Echo caught a glimpse of another airship's lights landing. The transport ship! It must be taking Lil away to Shark's Fin Peak or goodness knows where.

The *Scarlet Margaret* whirred away from Filigree Ridge until all the lights had completely disappeared. Echo shrank back behind the barrels as Bulkhead left the wheelhouse to throw down the anchor. With the ship secure, he lifted the hatch and disappeared back below decks. But panic still gripped Echo. She had spent her whole life searching for her mother before finally finding her. She couldn't lose Lil all over again. What if she needed help? Echo gazed across the deck and found herself staring at the cabinet on the forecastle where *Cloudcatcher* was stored. An idea started forming in her mind.

'Echo, you've gone very quiet,' whispered Horace.

'I'm thinking.'

'That's what I'm worried about.'

Echo didn't answer, but quietly pulled her boots on to her cold feet and laced them up, keeping her eyes on the cabinet all the while.

'Echo . . .'

Echo ignored him and crossed the deck.

'What are you doing?' hissed Horace.

'Nothing.'

'You're going to follow her, aren't you?'

Echo frowned. 'I have to.'

'Don't be stupid – you can't!'

'Lil's my *mother*.'

'I know she is.' Horace's face softened. 'But we're just children.'

'I'm a sky-pirate captain's daughter,' said Echo.

'But—'

'What if she's in danger?'

Horace shook his head. 'Bulkhead wouldn't have let her go alone if she was. And Lil would have told the rest of the crew what was going on if it was so important.'

Echo swallowed. Lil had been asked to go alone, and no one else knew that she was leaving. What if something did happen to her? No, it was no good. She had to follow Lil and make sure she was all right.

She opened the cabinet door.

'Echo, we don't even know how to fly *Cloudcatcher* properly.'

'*I* know how to do it.'

'It'll be dangerous.'

'I'm not scared of danger.'

'Maybe you should be. Sky pirates aren't to be trifled with.'

'I *am* a sky pirate,' Echo snapped. She dragged *Cloudcatcher* out on to the deck.

Horace folded his arms. 'Well, I'm not and I'm going back to bed.'

'So you won't come with me?' A flicker of fear ran through Echo, despite her best attempts to hide it. *What if I need your help?* she thought.

Horace twisted his hands together. 'Oh, Echo, you always

make me do this. This is supposed to be a holiday! I should be relaxing, not adventuring!'

Echo shrugged in a way she hoped looked nonchalant. 'Suit yourself. I'll adventure on my own.'

'But it's too dangerous to just fly off into the night alone!'

Echo grabbed the little bag of aethernets and stashed it under *Cloudcatcher*'s front seat. 'So come with me. Then I *won't* be alone.'

Horace's face was pale and pinched with worry. 'You don't have to do this to prove yourself.'

Echo shook her head. He was being ridiculous! Of course she didn't need to prove herself. She was doing this for Lil! 'You don't understand.' She crouched in front of *Cloudcatcher* and readied her hand on the starter handle. 'Are you with me or not?'

'I really don't think we should.'

'We're just going to take a look at the ice fortress. See what's really happening. Check Lil's safe.'

'Just one look?'

'Yes! To scope it out.'

'No danger?'

'No danger. We'll take a peek and come straight back again.'

Horace rubbed his upper arms nervously. 'I suppose it could be interesting. From a geological point of view, I mean. That mountain does have a very unusual rock formation. I heard about it once at a meeting of the Explorers' Guild in Port Tourbillon.'

'Exactly. Imagine how pleased the professor will be if you tell him you've seen it for real.'

'I really don't know.' Horace twisted his hands.

'Please, Horace.' Echo's voice softened. 'She's my mother and she's all alone. She didn't even take her cutlass.'

Horace puffed up his cheeks and blew out the air with a great sigh. 'Oh . . . okay then.' He scrambled up into the second seat and Echo's heart swelled as he did up his harness with a click. 'I know you're worried, Echo,' he said. 'It's not normal for a sky pirate like Lil to go anywhere unarmed, despite what the parrot's message said.'

Echo nodded. *Horace was right*, she thought, with a shiver. A sky pirate was never without their cutlass. And then something else suddenly occurred to her. *Stinger!*

'Wait, I forgot something. Be right back.' She jumped up and raced across the deck to the captain's quarters.

CHAPTER NINE

Silently, Echo eased open the door to the captain's quarters and crept inside. A board creaked under her boots and Gilbert's claws tightened on her shoulder. She froze for a moment, hardly daring to breathe. Had anyone heard her? But, after a few anxious moments, nobody came.

Echo tiptoed round to the other side of Lil's great oak desk. Gilbert leaped down on to the gleaming wooden surface and gave her a look that said, *Are you sure we should be sneaking around in here?*

It *did* feel strange to be on this side of the desk. Echo had only ever sat opposite Lil before, and her office was strictly out of bounds to the rest of the crew. A shiver of guilt ran through her. Gilbert was right: she shouldn't be in here. But what choice did she have? Lil wasn't here to ask. And what if she needed Echo? What if she'd got to Shark's Fin Peak and was already in trouble? No, sometimes a true sky pirate had to take matters into her own hands. Now, where was it?

Echo pulled open each of the drawers in turn, but there was no sign of *Stinger*.

'Where could she have hidden it, Gilbert?'

Echo gazed round the room in exasperation. It was so gloomy in here – the round portholes only let in a watery streak of moonlight and she didn't have anything with which to light an oil lamp.

Gilbert disappeared into the top drawer and Echo heard a dull *clink* as he butted something with his snout. An eerie green glow spilled out and Echo blinked in surprise, then laughed as she realized what Gilbert had found. 'A glow jar!' she said, taking the little glass container and swinging it from her finger. 'Well done, Gilbert! This'll come in handy.'

Gilbert popped his head out of the drawer with a chirrup that said, *You're welcome*, and scuttled back up on to Echo's shoulder.

'Now, let's find this sword.' Echo held up the jar to illuminate the room and straight away saw the sheathed sword lying on top of a hatbox on the map cabinet. She gazed up at it.

'Can you get it?' she said.

Gilbert bobbed his head, did a flying leap from Echo's shoulder and shimmied up the side of the cabinet in a flash of gold. At the top, he disappeared behind the scabbard. There was a scraping sound and suddenly the sheathed rapier was tipping and falling down into Echo's open arms.

Echo took the little sword in her right hand, feeling a tiny jolt of recognition as the hilt slipped into her palm perfectly. She slid *Stinger* into her belt, but even the slight weight of the blade made it slip out. Instead, she stashed it down the side of her boot, before scooping up Gilbert and racing to join Horace.

'What took you so long?' Horace grumbled, as she ran outside. He rubbed his folded arms. 'I was getting nervous out here.'

'Got my sword,' said Echo.

'Your ...' Horace's mouth gaped. 'But you're not ready! Flora said—'

'Yes, I am. We caught those crabs, didn't we?'

'But why would we need a sword, Echo? We're only going to take a look.'

'It's just a precaution,' said Echo, hoping he didn't notice she was lying. 'Here, I got something for you too. Catch.' She threw him the jar of glowbugs and scrambled into the seat, cranking *Cloudcatcher*'s engine into life. 'Ready?'

'Are you *sure* you know how to fly this thing without Bulkhead?'

'Of course!' Echo set her jaw. How hard could it be? She'd managed while Bulkhead was catching the clouds. And, although it seemed like a lifetime ago, she'd flown Professor

Daggerwing's airship in search of her mother twice, and only crashed it one of those times.

As Echo pulled back on the joysticks, Horace let out a squeal and covered both eyes with his hands.

Gilbert hid his face in the collar of Echo's shirt.

And *Cloudcatcher* whirred into the air.

Cloudcatcher purred silently through the indigo sky, Echo gripping the control handles and Horace staring grimly out. The air here was far colder than in Sleepy Palms and the wind's icy breath stung their cheeks. She squinted into the darkness. The transport ship had left Filigree Ridge and they had now been trailing it for nearly an hour.

'Not too close,' hissed Horace.

'Don't panic,' said Echo. 'They won't spot us without our lights on.' Even so, she took the vehicle a little higher up in the clouds, out of the sightline of the other ship.

'They're slowing,' she said. 'Are we nearly . . . Oh!'

The clouds parted to reveal a bright full moon and Echo gasped as Shark's Fin Peak suddenly appeared before them. Its rocky surface curved in an arc, looming over all the other mountains in the range, its pointed peak higher even than the clouds.

'Well, I can see why it's called Shark's Fin Peak,' said Horace. 'It's just like the dorsal fin of a Great Grey. Look at that rock formation!' He leaned forward in awe, then sat back and folded his arms as if suddenly remembering why they were here. He turned to Echo. 'Can we go back now? We know they've taken her where they said they would.'

Echo shook her head. 'I need to make sure she's safe.'

'But what are we going to do if she isn't? We're just children.'

'We've brought a getaway vehicle.' Echo circled *Cloudcatcher* away from a searchlight that shone out in a yellowish beam through the clouds. 'We just need to find somewhere to land it.'

'There won't be anywhere. The postal parrot said it's an ice fortress! They're not generally easy to get into.'

'Hold this steady,' Echo said, swivelling the control handles so he could reach them.

She picked up Horace's spyglass and scanned the mountain. The fortress was a castle of gleaming white ice carved into the rock face, with a skinny tower that soared skywards and window slits that glowed with a flickering blueish light. The arched face of the mountain that the fortress clung to was almost sheer, with no obvious route in or out that Echo could see, other than the airship landing pad, which was lit with floodlights.

She saw guards armed with flintlock pistols and shaggy grey dogs patrolling the perimeter. She wouldn't tell Horace about those, not yet at least.

'We'll have to try the other side,' she said brightly. 'There must be somewhere we can stash *Cloudcatcher.*'

'Even if we do, how are we going to get inside?' Horace's voice shook. 'You never think of these things, Echo.'

'We'll work it out when we get there,' said Echo, ignoring the way her hands were shaking as she took back the controls. They could figure out a way to get past the guards, but first they had to find somewhere to land. She wheeled the little vehicle about and they soared in a loop round the mountain's curved peak, away from the floodlights and the fortress itself.

'It's impenetrable,' said Horace glumly. 'Oh, please can we go back, Echo? You said we would!'

'Nothing's impenetrable,' said Echo, snatching a guilty glance at Horace's forlorn face. She was breaking her promise to him, but she couldn't leave Lil here unarmed and alone. Not now she'd seen how heavily guarded the place was. What if her mother never came back?

Echo scanned the peak with renewed focus. 'We just need to try harder. Look – over there!'

Tucked in the curve of the mountain beneath the fortress was a little cave, just out of sight of the searchlights. Echo's heart lifted. It was the perfect place to land unseen. The landing would be tricky, but she was prepared to take the chance.

Echo gripped the controls, set her jaw and took *Cloudcatcher* down on to Shark's Fin Peak.

CHAPTER TEN

As Echo guided *Cloudcatcher* closer to the small cave, a curtain of freezing sleet blew slantwise at them, almost knocking the little vessel off course. *Cloudcatcher* bobbed and bumped on the wind, tipping this way and then that, Echo shielding her eyes with one hand, and steering with the other. She could just about make out the cave entrance in the moonlight. Then a cloud went across and she was flying in near-darkness.

'Oh help!' squealed Horace, hiding his face in his hands. 'We're going to crash!'

Gilbert's scales turned white, and he plunged head first into Echo's pocket.

'It's fine ... we're nearly—' But Echo didn't finish her sentence as *Cloudcatcher* made contact with the ground and skidded sideways into the cave opening.

'—down,' she panted, as the propeller slowed to a halt and they found themselves askew in a snowdrift.

Once they'd got their breath back, Echo clicked open her safety harness and jumped down from *Cloudcatcher*, almost losing her footing as she skidded on the icy ground.

Horace got down warily beside her. 'I really don't think we should be doing this, Echo.'

'I need to make sure she's all right.'

'But you said we were just going to look.'

Echo sighed. 'I know – I'm sorry. But we're here now and I can't just let her disappear. What if she needs us? Bulkhead said she was tricked before. What if it's happening again?'

Horace shook his head and pressed his lips together in a tight line.

Echo turned away, guilt settling in her belly, and gazed up at the fortress above. What would be waiting for them up there? Flora had said there were seven sky-pirate clans, but other than that Echo didn't have a clue.

She frowned. 'Now, how are we going to get up there?'

'Echo, please. We can't!' Horace folded his arms tightly across his chest.

'We just need to go a little closer.'

Horace huffed. 'Well, I'm waiting here.'

'Fine.' Echo left the cave and set out up the slope, but the surface was so icy her feet slipped backwards two paces for every one she took forward. After a few minutes of struggling, she still hadn't made much progress. She paused for a breather and glared up at the fortress.

In the distance, there was the howl of a wolf and a sudden scrabbling behind her made Echo jump. She turned to find Horace hotfooting it towards her. 'Changed my mind,' he puffed. 'We should stick together.'

After several more minutes of slipping and sliding, they hadn't got much further. Echo looked up at the fortress again, but it was still just as far away as ever.

'I can see why they don't bother guarding this side,' puffed Horace. He stopped for a moment, steadying his hands on his knees, and gazed up in defeat at the fortress clinging to the rock face above them. 'We're never going to get up there at this rate. Are you sure you don't want to turn back?'

Echo shook her head, refusing to be beaten. 'There must be a way. We need something to pull ourselves up with.'

Horace rolled his eyes. 'I'm afraid I didn't bring my crampons.'

'There has to be something we can use.' Echo looked back at *Cloudcatcher*, but the little vehicle was bare and empty.

There was a flicker of lightning somewhere in the distance, followed a few seconds later by a rumble of thunder that reverberated through the mountains. Thunderclouds! That was it! Echo scrambled and slid back down the slope to *Cloudcatcher*.

'What are you doing now?' said Horace.

'Just getting this,' said Echo, reaching under her seat to grab the bag of aethernets. She couldn't see them, but, as she dug her hand in, she could feel the tingle of invisible fibres running through her fingers. She lurched her way back to Horace. 'The aethernets,' she said. 'We'll throw one out and hook it on to something.'

She glanced up at the snow-covered slope, squinting against the icy wind. Several metres above them, some greyish rocks thrust out through the snow. 'There.'

'Do you think it's strong enough?' Horace eyed it warily.

'If an aethernet can hold a thundercloud, it can hold two children,' said Echo in her most convincing voice.

Horace cast an anxious glance behind them. 'What if it snaps or something?'

Echo tried to push down the worries that niggled at her. She needed to know that Lil was okay and, if she thought too long about it, she'd never be brave enough. She set her jaw. 'It won't,' she said firmly, whirling the net round her head.

Once, twice . . . and throw.

She couldn't see where it had landed, but, when she pulled the net tight, it held. It must have caught on a rocky outcrop up ahead.

'Come on,' she said. 'Hold on to me.'

'Are we nearly there?' whimpered Horace. 'I don't think I can hang on much longer.'

Echo's feet scrabbled for purchase on the ice as she hauled

herself up the slope, hand over hand. Her flimsy layers of Sleepy Palms clothes suddenly felt insubstantial in the biting wind and she began to shiver. Worry crept through her. Were they out of their depth? She grimaced. Yes, they were, but they were here now and she couldn't let Horace know how scared she was. Echo gazed up at the rocky outcrop, which still seemed impossibly far away.

'Not much further,' she said through gritted teeth. 'Come on, we can do it. One step at a time.' The muscles in her arms burned as she pulled herself up the rock face with new vigour.

A sudden gust of wind almost knocked them both off balance and blew an icy flurry of snow into Echo's face. But she screwed her eyes shut against the cold and kept moving, slowly, one hand after another, up the slope.

After what seemed like a lifetime, Echo finally managed to grasp hold of the jutting rock. She heaved herself over it and lay panting on the ice as Horace dragged himself up beside her.

'We made it,' she gasped, rubbing the ice from her eyelashes and looking around. The fortress wall lay up ahead of them. 'That's where we need to go.'

Horace followed her gaze. 'But, Echo . . .'

'What now?' groaned Echo in exasperation. 'I do wish you'd stop complaining.'

'But, Echo, look.' Horace held out a shaking finger.

She looked up. 'Oh.'

Four guard dogs were hurtling towards them across the snow, teeth bared.

'Oh no . . .'

'Aaagh!' squeaked Horace, edging backwards and almost toppling down the icy slope.

'Wait,' said Echo, telling herself to stay calm, despite her thudding heart. She took a deep, shaky breath. 'Shouldn't we stand our ground or something?'

'I don't know!'

'You're supposed to be the zoological expert.'

'I study insects, not . . . not wolves!' Horace clung to her sleeve tightly. 'Oh, we're going to die – I just know it! We'll be savaged! We're—'

'Shh!'

The dogs slowed to a trot, then slunk forward, snarling. Echo saw shark-tooth collars round their muscular necks and a horrible thought occurred to her. Shark's Fin Peak. Shark-tooth collars. Could the fortress be the home of the Thunder Sharks? The worst of all the sky-pirate clans, with a tank of hungry sharks in the hold of their ship? Terror swirled in her stomach and she froze.

'Echo,' squeaked Horace, clutching her hand. 'They're coming closer.'

'Nice doggies,' she said, her voice trembling. 'Easy now.'

She glanced sideways at Horace. 'Any ideas?'

Without taking his eyes off the dogs, Horace gave a quick shake of his head.

The lead dog snarled, its grey pelt bristling, and Echo caught a glimpse of sharp yellow teeth and lurid pink gums. She swallowed and stepped back, teetering on the edge of the outcrop. If they dropped down the slope, would the aethernet hold them? Perhaps, but then what? The dogs were bound to be more sure-footed than she and Horace were. What if they followed? Would running away make them attack? She glanced around in desperation.

'Hey! Lucas, Zephyr, Mungo!' A figure appeared round the fortress wall, indistinct in the snow.

The dogs all turned their heads.

'What you got for me, lads?' As the figure jogged towards them, Echo realized with relief that it was a boy not much older than her and Horace.

He put something small and metallic to his lips and blew. There was no sound, but the dogs stopped in their tracks, cocking their ears towards the boy.

Inside Echo's jerkin, Gilbert squirmed.

The boy ran forward, pushing his way between the dogs and stopping before Echo and Horace. 'You're . . . you're children!'

Echo licked her lips and nodded.

'Who are you? What're you doing on Shark's Fin Peak?'

Echo thought quickly. The boy was about as tall as she was, with bright blue eyes and curly ginger hair. He wore a coat of raggedy blue furs, navy leather boots and a shark-tooth collar round his neck. More shark teeth! She swallowed. He had to be one of the fearsome Thunder Sharks, or one of their minions. Was he dangerous? She took in the shiny little whistle that he still held close to his lips. The dogs certainly were.

Echo thought quickly. Telling the truth wasn't an option – she'd just have to make something up.

'We're lost,' she said finally, gesturing back down to where *Cloudcatcher* lay askew in the cave mouth. 'We crashed our machine.'

The landing had been pretty shaky, so it was *almost* true, she thought, crossing her fingers behind her back.

The boy narrowed his eyes. 'On the night of the alliance meeting? Bit of a coincidence.'

'We were searching for thunderclouds,' said Horace, his voice squeaking.

Echo shot him an admiring glance. Good old Horace! She knew he'd come in useful.

Horace went on. 'We have this special net, you see. It's made of spider silk—'

'You got an aethernet?' The boy stepped forward, his blue eyes wide. 'Show me!'

Horace looked at Echo nervously. She frowned. This could be bad. 'Why are you so interested?' she said, folding her arms.

'I 'eard about 'em, but I ain't ever seen one,' said the boy. 'My dad told me about 'em once, before I came here, of course.' His face dropped a little at the memory.

'Don't you like being here?' asked Echo, sensing a way in.

'Don't get no choice,' said the boy, shrugging, his veneer of toughness suddenly looking thin. 'My dad lost me in a game of grog rummy. They say the Thunder Sharks are card sharks too, and they're right!' He gave a hollow laugh. 'So now I work for 'em.'

Echo nodded slowly. So she was right: this was the Thunder Sharks' lair. 'If we show you our aethernet, what will you do for us? Will you help us get inside?'

'Inside?' The boy stared at her. 'What do you wanna do that for? You know all seven of the sky-pirate clan leaders are in there?'

'Of course I know.' Echo squared her shoulders, forgetting she was supposed to be lost for a moment. 'I'm a sky pirate too.'

'Yeah, right!' The boy grinned, then his smile slipped as he took in Echo's fierce expression.

He licked his lips and nodded. 'I suppose I could

show you the way in.'

'We just want to hear what's said at the meeting,' said Echo. 'Do you know where they're gathering?' *Or who they all are*, she thought, though she didn't want to give away how little she actually knew about the alliance.

The boy nodded and looked up at the fortress. 'The septagonal hall,' he said, gesturing up at a circular room at the top of the main tower, where lights flickered from the high, arched windows. 'That's where all the meetings of the Seven Skies Alliance are held.'

'And could you get us in there?'

The boy bit his lip. 'It'd be difficult.'

Echo nodded. 'What if we give you our aethernet?'

'Echo!' Horace nudged her. 'We can't give it to him.'

Echo silenced him with a look. 'It's very valuable, I know,' she said. 'But so is getting into that room.'

'But—'

'Trust me, Horace.' Echo reached into her left pocket and drew out her empty hand. 'See this?' she said.

The boy squinted at her hand. 'N . . . no.'

'Exactly. You can't.' Echo smiled. 'Aethernets are so fine that they're invisible to the naked eye. But you can feel them. Put out your hand.'

The boy uncertainly thrust out a dirty palm and shuffled closer to her. The dogs looked from Echo to him expectantly, still drooling and looking like they might pounce at any moment. Echo held her nerve. She dropped the imaginary net into the boy's hand.

'Feel that?' she said.

The boy frowned. 'No, not really . . .'

'Concentrate,' said Echo. 'It's incredibly fine, so fine you can barely sense it. In fact, only the most sensitive people can.'

'I don't know.' He frowned again.

'Well, I might as well take it back then,' said Echo, folding her arms. 'If you can't tell when you're holding it, there's no point me giving it to you.' She reached for the boy's palm, but he closed his fingers and snatched his hand away.

'No, I can feel it. I definitely can.' His brow furrowed with uncertainty.

'Really?' Echo said. 'Because if you're not sure I'll have it back.'

'I'm sure.' A grin spread across the boy's face. 'Thank you, er . . .'

'Echo,' said Echo. 'And this is Horace.'

'I'm Grub,' said the boy, carefully depositing the imaginary net into the pocket of his breeches. 'Come on. There's a back door. Follow me.'

Grub blew his silent whistle again and the dogs ran on ahead. Echo and Horace followed them along a narrow ledge that curved round the mountain, keeping pressed close to the cliffside and not daring to look down to their right at the sheer drop.

As they rounded the corner to the rear of the fortress, Grub suddenly stopped and took out a glowbug-powered lantern.

'This is the emergency exit,' he said, pointing to what at first appeared to be a blank white wall. When Echo looked closely, she saw the outline of a small door cut into the ice. 'Any trouble, and we slip out here to the sledges.'

'Sledges?' said Echo, looking around.

Grub raised his lantern and pointed to a heap of wooden sledges that lay higgledy-piggledy by the icy mouth of a tunnel cut into the rock. 'Goes right through the mountain to the aerodock. Perfect if we're ambushed.' He took a bunch of keys from his pocket, unlocked the door, which opened silently, and ushered them inside.

Echo followed him into a dimly lit corridor with walls of gleaming ice. It was almost as cold inside as outside and she huffed out a white cloud with every breath. White torches hung from the walls and in the strange blueish light the floor glistened with frost.

'We'll need to be quick,' said Grub. 'Old Gus is on the aerodock, receiving the guests, but once they're all here they'll gather upstairs in the chamber.'

Old Gus! Echo recognized that name. Was he the one Bulkhead had warned her mother about? A flicker of fear ran through her.

'Show us where it is,' said Echo, trying to stop her teeth from chattering. She didn't know if it was the cold or the sense of dread creeping through her bones that was making her hands shake, but she clenched them into fists and stuffed them into her pockets until they were almost steady.

'This way.' After leading them down numerous winding passages, Grub opened another door, this one carved of ice, and ushered them up a narrow spiral staircase. Their footsteps rang out as they hurried upwards and followed Grub to the top of the tower, where a wide door of gleaming crystal barred their way.

'In here,' whispered Grub, pushing it open and ushering them through. He looked over his shoulder and Echo saw his face was pinched with fear. 'I've gotta go. If Old Gus catches me, I dunno what he'll do.'

'Thanks,' whispered Echo, but Grub had already scuttled back down the stairway, his blue furs flapping, leaving Horace and Echo alone in the entrance to the septagonal hall.

CHAPTER ELEVEN

Echo turned and entered the circular room, her eyes widening as she took in the seven-sided table inlaid with a shimmering mother-of-pearl map. 'Look,' she breathed, stepping forward and running her hands over the smooth surface in wonder. Everything was there – Port Tourbillon, the Violet Isles, Dark Nordland. Gilbert scuttled down her arm and landed neatly on the table, cocking his head to look. The map was divided by pearly lines that criss-crossed the surface from each corner of the table.

'What do you think this means?' Echo counted seven sections dividing the map. Seven sections for seven sky-pirate clans. 'Perhaps this is how they divide the territory up between them?' she said.

'There's no time to look at that,' said Horace, glancing anxiously round the room. 'There'll be here any minute. Where are we going to hide?'

'They won't be here just yet. Old Gus is still at the aerodock.' Echo examined the table further and took in an inscription: THE SEVEN SKIES. She stared at the shimmering map. But which part belonged to the Black Sky Wolves?

'Maybe we could hide here if we drew the curtains?' said Horace, gesturing to a window seat carved out of the icy walls and covered in rough sackcloth cushions.

Echo looked over and nodded, then turned back to the map, still unable to tear herself away. This was real sky-pirate business! Each of the seven places at the table had its own ebony-dark wooden chair and, as she looked closely, she saw that the back of each one was carved with a different emblem. There was a shark – that had to be for the Thunder Sharks – a snake, a bolt of lightning. She circled the table, looking at each one in turn. 'This must be where my mother sits,' she said, running her fingers over the snarling wolf's head carved into the back of the furthest seat.

Gilbert raised his crest in warning as the faint jingle of many pairs of sky-pirate boots echoed up the icy stairwell.

'Echo! They're coming!' hissed Horace.

Echo took one last glance at the map before running round the table and slipping in beside Horace on the window seat. They shrank back behind the curtain as the footsteps grew louder. After a moment, Echo heard the door creak open and a mixture of rough voices spilled through. She dared to inch back the curtain a fraction. In the blueish light of the flickering torches, she saw the seven pirate captains enter and take their seats.

Lil was at the far side of the table, in the chair Echo had identified. Her face was an eerie mask, almost unrecognizable, with thick stripes of indigo clay smeared on her cheeks and her tricorne hat casting strange shadows on her features. Next to her was a man with a shock of spiky hair as yellow as his jerkin and one mechanical eye that zoomed in and out as he gazed about the room. On her other side was an almond-eyed woman in bright orange robes, with armfuls of jangling golden bangles and red-painted lips, her black hair drawn into a tight knot atop her head, a jewelled dagger skewered through it.

Another sky pirate stood with his blue-fur-clad back to them, his shaggy grey hair twisted into beaded ropes beneath his tricorne. He took a seat in the shark chair, his back to the window seat where the two children were hidden. The hairs on the back of Echo's neck stood up and she shrank back further behind the drapes. So *this* was the terrible Old Gus.

'Welcome to this meetin' of the Seven Skies Alliance,' said the man in a voice like gravel. 'And welcome to Shark's Fin Peak. I'm sure I don't need to remind yer that, under the Treaty of the Seven Skies, no weapons are permitted and every pirate may speak freely.' He raised his tankard of grog. 'Live by the sky, die by the sky!'

'Live by the sky, die by the sky!' echoed the others, raising their own glasses. Echo strained to get a look at them all, but most of their faces were hidden in shadows and Old Gus still had his back to them. Echo's jaw clenched in frustration. If only she could get a better view! She shifted in her hiding place and almost toppled forward, grabbing on to the edge of the window seat just in time.

Horace's eyes widened in horror and Echo grimaced. It would be bad enough if her own mother found her here, let alone a whole roomful of the most fearsome sky-pirate leaders! She sat back down and bit her lip, promising herself that, even if she didn't get to see much, she would at least remember everything that was said.

'Now, yer might be wonderin' why I called this meetin'.' Old Gus put his tankard down for a moment. 'Grub!' he yelled over his shoulder. 'Where yer got to? Do I 'ave to come and wring yer scrawny neck—?'

There was a crash from outside and then Grub came struggling through the doors with his arms wrapped round something large and heavy-looking, concealed beneath a navy velvet drape. 'S . . . sorry, Cap'n.' He put the contraption down on the table with some difficulty, then retreated backwards from the room.

Old Gus cleared his throat and drew back the velvet covering.

Echo squirmed and craned her neck to see what Grub had placed on the table. 'What is it?' she whispered to Horace.

'Looks like some kind of metal creature,' murmured Horace, peeking through a gap in the curtain.

Gilbert braced himself on Echo's shoulder to take a look too.

Echo peered out, but Old Gus's bulk concealed whatever it was that the others were all staring at. What she could see, however, was the surprise on their faces as they leaned forward. The man with the robotic eye was zooming in and out to study it. And, although Echo could see that Lil was trying not to show it, her mother's brow was creased with worry.

'The septopus,' said Old Gus. 'It's been a long time since we've needed to use it.'

A murmur went round the room and, as the pirate shifted, Echo caught a glimpse of a metallic, seven-tentacled creature with a bulbous head in the centre of the table.

'As yer all know, Sabre-toothed Sascha died several months ago, after fallin' into a pit o' vipers.'

There were murmurs of, 'May she rest in peace,' from the other pirate captains, and Old Gus removed his tricorne hat and bowed his head.

'May she rest in peace,' he repeated, and cleared his throat. 'Before she died so tragically, she left a message for the remainin' pirates of the Seven Skies Alliance, but on condition that all of us 'ad to be 'ere to receive it. So she sealed it in the septopus, as is tradition.'

'What message?' said a dark-skinned pirate with hair in long locs and a red jerkin encrusted with jewels, who sat with his back to Echo.

In answer, Old Gus leaned forward and turned a small

wheel on the head of the septopus. 'Everyone remember what to do? State yer name and yer faction, and give yer fingerprint.' He sat down.

In the centre of the table, the septopus began to slowly turn before stopping and extending a tentacle to him. He placed his forefinger on to the sucker, which glowed red.

'Old Gus of the Thunder Sharks,' he said.

Cogs whirred and the red-lit sucker turned green. The septopus's head swivelled round to face the next pirate, a woman with fiery red hair and a green cloak, who stretched out one elegant green-nailed hand.

'Miranda Vossberg of the Scurvy Sea Snakes.'

The septopus turned again.

'Ozwald the Terrible of the Pitiless Plunderers,' said the man in the red jerkin with his back to Echo.

'Madame Maja of the Darkhearts,' said the orange-robed woman, her bangles jangling as she reached out to place her fingertip on the mechanical creature's tentacle.

Another tentacle unfurled as Lil gruffly said her name. Echo's scalp prickled as Lil extended her hand and placed her finger on the tentacle. She held her breath as the cogs whirred. Finally, the sucker lit green and Echo exhaled.

So far so good. Lil didn't seem to be in any trouble yet, but Echo still needed to be on high alert. She put her hand to *Stinger*'s hilt.

The sky pirates continued round the table. 'Steel-eyed

Seth of the Stormshakers,' said the man in yellow with the mechanical eye.

Finally, the septopus extended its seventh tentacle to the last pirate. All Echo could see of her was her deep purple waistcoat and the shiny black plait snaking down her back. 'Rashmi the Ruthless of the Heartless Violet Pilots,' she said.

Echo held her breath as the septopus's head rotated, slowly at first, then faster and faster, until it finally opened like a flower to reveal a small envelope sealed with a shiny blob of black wax.

For a moment, the pirates all sat in silence, then Rashmi the Ruthless lunged forward to grab it.

'Hey!' yelled Steel-eyed Seth, his eye whizzing in and out in fury. 'What d'you think you're doing?'

'Someone's got to read it,' said Rashmi, with a shrug of one velvet-clad shoulder.

'And why should it be you?' Miranda Vossberg gave Rashmi an icy glare.

'*I* should read it.' Madame Maja made a grab for the envelope, but Rashmi elegantly moved out of her way.

'Someone just read it!' Ozwald the Terrible banged his fist on the table, his locs jumping in rage.

'ENOUGH!' yelled Old Gus. 'Remember the terms of the treaty. There's no fightin' at an alliance meetin'.' He smiled nastily. 'We'll save that for later.'

'But—' started Steel-eyed Seth.

'And anyone who forgets 'ow to behave will get marched on to *Obsidian* and fed to my shark,' added Old Gus.

A hush gathered over the pirates as they sat back down, still glaring at one another.

Rashmi tossed her plait over her shoulder and ran one sharp violet-lacquered fingernail under the seal, releasing it with a papery rasp.

Echo held her breath as the pirate captain pulled out a crisp piece of cream-coloured parchment and began to read.

'To the members of the Seven Skies Alliance. I spent my life searching for treasure, but never once did I manage to find the Cutlass of Calinthe.'

A surprised murmur went round the room.

'But the Cutlass of Calinthe was destroyed,' said Lil, her face ashen.

'Let me finish,' Rashmi snarled. She cleared her throat and continued to read. 'When Indigo Vi vanquished Calinthe Casterbrook, she hurled the cutlass into the flames of Mount Flameflux and we all thought it had been destroyed for ever. But I have since found out that there was a dragon nesting in that volcano. That dragon escaped with the cutlass and took it for its own treasure hoard. The Cutlass of Calinthe remains intact.'

A gasp erupted round the table.

Rashmi continued. 'I am too old and ill now to chase after it, but I have found out where it lies. I have drawn a map that shows the exact location of the dragon's new lair. Whoever can solve my riddle, find the map and retrieve the cutlass first is its rightful owner and leader of all the seven skies.'

A hush descended on the room and the sky pirates shot fierce glances at one another.

Rashmi paused for a moment and then continued to read silently.

Gilbert tensed on Echo's shoulder. She snuck a glance at Horace, whose face was pale in the moonlight. What did it mean? Leader of all the seven skies? Did that mean if the Black Sky Wolves found this fabled cutlass, Lil would be a sky-pirate queen? Echo's insides fizzed with excitement. Dragon lairs! Legendary treasure! This would be their biggest adventure yet!

'Oi, read it out loud so we can all hear!' yelled Ozwald the Terrible.

Rashmi cleared her throat.

> 'To find the way to dragon caves,
> Seek knowledge underneath the waves.
> For seventy rungs you'll need to climb,
> If you're to find the map in time.
> Face up to me and hold my hand,
> A trio and quarter's the place to land.'

After a moment of silence, the rest of the pirates all got to their feet and made for the door, looking daggers at one another.

As they disappeared down the stairs and their voices and

footsteps faded, Echo sank back on her heels. What did the riddle mean? She bit her lip and waited until the heavy-booted footsteps died away at the bottom of the staircase before flinging aside the curtain and uncoiling herself from their hiding place.

'Come on,' she said to Horace. 'We've got to get back to the *Scarlet Margaret*. There's a cutlass and dragon treasure to find!'

'Dragons,' said Horace, with a shiver. 'I don't like the sound of that.'

'Lil will know what to do,' said Echo. 'I bet she's solved the riddle already. Come on, back to *Cloudcatcher*.'

'Finally, you're saying something sensible,' said Horace, hugging himself. 'The sooner we're back on the *Scarlet Margaret*, the better.'

Echo took one last look at the septopus before easing the door open. She listened for a moment, then crept back down the stairs. There was no sign of Grub, but that was just as well thought Echo guiltily. After all, he was bound to realize the aethernet she'd given him wasn't real sooner or later, and they needed to be long gone by the time he did.

They made their way back through the snaking corridors to the door that led out on to the ice.

'What about the dogs?' hissed Horace, as Echo pushed the door open. But there were no dogs or people to be seen on the path.

'Come on,' said Echo. 'We've got lucky.' They hurried round

the corner. 'We'll have to go down backwards with the net again,' she said, pulling it out of her knapsack and fastening one end to the rocks.

'Er . . . Echo.'

'What?' she said without looking up.

'Where did we leave *Cloudcatcher*?'

Echo jerked her head up, taking in Horace's ghost-white face and following his gaze down the mountain. Fear rippled through her.

Cloudcatcher had disappeared.

CHAPTER TWELVE

'Where is it?' Echo frowned in confusion and leaned as far as she dared over the edge of the icy slope. She peered through the white flurries of snow. It must be hidden under the snowdrifts. After all, it had to be there somewhere! But, however hard she looked, she just couldn't see the little machine. She swallowed the lump of panic that had formed in her throat. What could have happened to *Cloudcatcher*?

Horace pulled the spyglass from his satchel and peered around. After a moment, he took a deep, shuddering breath. 'I think I can see it.'

'Where?'

He silently pointed down the mountain and passed the spyglass to Echo.

As she put it to her eye, her heart dropped. There was a trail of blackened snow and debris where something had fallen and skidded down the mountainside. She followed the trail and saw *Cloudcatcher*, or what remained of *Cloudcatcher*, lying upside down in a crevasse. She bit her lip. It was unreachable and, even if they could get to it, the propeller was clearly bent out of shape. No, the little vessel was damaged beyond repair.

Echo put down the spyglass and looked at Horace, whose face was almost as white as the snow that was falling.

'What are we going to do?' he whimpered. 'How will we ever get back to the *Scarlet Margaret*?'

'I don't know.' What *would* they do? Echo frowned and looked around for something – anything – that might help her. How could she have been so stupid! Lil had been perfectly fine without her, and now they were stranded here, without *Cloudcatcher* and without a plan. Lil would be furious when they got back to the *Scarlet Margaret*. If they ever did get back.

'Echo, there's no way off this mountain except by air, and our only vessel's ...' Horace trailed off and took a deep, tearful breath.

'Maybe that's it,' said Echo, frowning in thought. If the only way off Shark's Fin Peak was by airship, then that was how they had to leave, and there wasn't much time if they were going to catch up with Lil. She shoved the aethernet and spyglass back into her knapsack. 'We need to get to the aerodock.'

Echo and Horace retraced their steps to the icy tunnel and its heap of ancient-looking wooden sledges.

Horace eyed them nervously. 'I'm not sure about this, Echo. Who even knows where the tunnel comes out?'

'Grub said it leads to the aerodock.'

Echo peered into the tunnel. It was lit with the same strange blueish lights as the fortress, but, as it curved its way through the heart of the mountain, the exit wasn't visible. Doubt gripped her. They could be sliding straight into danger. But she had to find Lil and get them back to the *Scarlet Margaret*. She took a deep breath. It was this or freeze on Shark's Fin Peak.

'Come on.' She nudged Horace into one of the sledges, got in the front seat and grabbed the ropes with both hands. 'Here we go.'

Echo pushed away with one foot and the sledge slowly slid forward into the icy tunnel. She braced both feet against it as they picked up speed, and soon they were whizzing soundlessly on the slick ice through the very heart of the mountain.

Faster and faster they went, until the sides of the tunnel were just a blur and the ice-cold wind made Echo's cheeks numb.

'Oh help,' whimpered Horace, as they careered ever more wildly through the ice tunnel.

Echo blinked tears out of her eyes to see yellowish lights up ahead. They were approaching the opening to the aerodock. They had to slow down! She glanced down to find a brake, and realized there wasn't one. 'How do we stop this thing?' she muttered.

'I thought you were driving!' Horace squealed.

'Stick your foot out!' Echo thrust both her booted feet out to slow them down, sending a spray of ice up into the air.

'Aaagh!' yelped Horace, as the sledge skidded sideways across the ice and thudded heavily into the side of the tunnel, rolling over three times before finally tipping them out into the snow.

They lay for a moment, panting, then sat up.

'Well, I guess that's one way of doing it,' Horace said. 'What now?'

'The aerodock,' said Echo. 'Let's find Lil and get out of here.'

As they crept towards the tunnel mouth, Echo heard rough voices up ahead. She peered out round a large boulder and her heart clenched with worry as she saw the aerodock was empty, save for one ship. In the distance, the lights of the last transport ships were disappearing into the night. So Lil had gone. Echo's lip trembled. She had hoped beyond anything that Lil would still be here, that she'd be able to explain what had happened and Lil would have taken them back to the *Scarlet Margaret* with her. But her hopes had been dashed.

Echo rubbed her eyes on her sleeve and forced her mouth into a firm line. She couldn't let Horace see how scared she was, or he'd panic and they'd never get out of here.

She scanned the aerodock again. The remaining ship was shaped like a great black shark, with a charcoal-grey balloon envelope bobbing above it. That had to be the Thunder Sharks' own airship. All the other sky-pirate leaders seemed to have left, but the whole dock was still abuzz with activity.

Horace peered out too. 'They look like they're about to go.'

Echo nodded. Horace was right: they did seem as if they'd leave at any moment now that the race was on for the treasure. Blue-fur-clad sky pirates ran here and there, loading up the ship with barrels and crates. One buck-toothed boy dangled from ropes to inspect the balloon, while two more polished the portholes and a girl with her hair in a thick blonde plait oiled the tail-shaped rudder.

Echo straightened herself up. Maybe there was a chance for them to get away. 'We have to get onboard,' she said.

'Onboard! We *can't*!' Horace gasped.

'We'll sneak on. They won't see us.'

'But we don't even know where they're going.'

'It doesn't matter,' said Echo, already creeping forward, her heart pounding.

'B . . . but what if they take us even further away from the *Scarlet Margaret*?' Horace whispered.

'They're going to find the first clue,' said Echo, thinking out loud, but trying to sound as if she had some kind of plan. 'And that's on land somewhere. If we can stow away, we can escape and run for help when they get there.'

'If you say so.' Horace wrapped his arms round himself in a hug, his teeth chattering.

'Do you have a better idea? We can't stay here.'

'Fine.'

Echo turned back to the airship and kept going. As they crept closer, Echo saw a plaque on one flank that read OBSIDIAN. She and Horace watched in silence as the front section of the ship opened like a great set of jaws. A waiting sky pirate, with the blue-fur uniform of the Thunder Sharks and a lurid red scar zigzagging down one cheek, hefted his barrel under one bulging arm and marched onboard.

'That's our way in,' said Echo.

'There!' Horace shook his head. 'Oh no, Echo! We can't! Not right at the front!'

'We can't climb up the ladder; we've got no idea what we'll find at the top and we'll be too exposed. The hold's the best place to hide.'

Horace nodded stiffly. 'Okay, I suppose—'

'Shh.' Echo quietened him with a wave as the sky pirate with the scar emerged from the ship's jaws empty-handed and returned to the main entrance of the fortress, with its tall silver portcullis. 'Now!'

She ran forward, keeping to the shadows, with Horace close beside her. There was a clatter from behind them just as they reached the ramp and they ducked below it as another pirate approached. The gangplank rumbled above them as she stomped her way onboard. As they waited for her to re-emerge, Echo took in Horace's stricken face. Was this really going to work? She steeled herself. It had to. There was no other way back. Lil and the others had no idea where she and Horace were. And, if *Obsidian* left Shark's Fin Peak too, they really would be stranded on a mountain of ice with no way home. This was the only way out.

She waited until the pirate had stamped back down the gangplank. 'Come on,' she whispered to Horace, and they heaved themselves on to the gangplank and into *Obsidian*'s gaping mouth.

Echo scurried into the ship's hold, where she ducked behind a crate marked SKY BISCUITS, pulling Horace behind her. They were just in time, as more footsteps heralded the arrival of another group of barrel-rolling pirates.

Echo and Horace were deep in *Obsidian*'s windowless belly and Echo had to blink as her eyes adjusted to the gloom. As she did so, she saw that the hold was packed with weapons, barrels of gunpowder, boxes marked HATCHETS and CROSSBOWS and a huge crate that said **SHARK CHOW** in lurid red letters.

Echo remembered with horror Flora's tales of the Thunder Sharks. *They say their leader, Old Gus, keeps a shark tank in the hold of their ship. And if someone crosses him . . . he feeds them to the sharks!* Was there really a tank of ferocious creatures down here? She glanced around nervously, then shrank back further as the footsteps got closer.

'Reckon we're ready?' asked a gruff woman's voice.

'Ready enough,' said a man. 'Old Gus wants to leave pronto. Get a head start on the others.'

'That's assuming they haven't left already.'

'They've gotta get back to their crews first, remember?'

Echo's heart twisted as she thought of Lil heading back to the *Scarlet Margaret* without them. When would she notice Echo was gone? Would she look in her cabin when she returned from Shark's Fin Peak in the morning? Echo bit her lip with worry. They'd just have to get back before then. They'd be in with a chance if they ended up somewhere near Sleepy Palms.

Echo jumped at the sound of something heavy being hefted, the floor reverberating with the weight of it.

'That's it then,' said the woman. 'Onward to the Aqualiber Vaults.'

The Aqualiber Vaults? Echo wracked her brains, but she couldn't remember ever seeing that name on any of Lil's charts, or Professor Daggerwing's map back in Port Tourbillon.

She looked over at Horace, but he shrugged and looked as mystified as she was.

'Let's close her up,' said the man.

The footsteps faded away down the gangplank again, then there was a clank, and a grinding sound, and the little light there was gradually dwindled to a sliver, before disappearing completely and leaving Echo and Horace alone in the gloom.

'Echo, I don't like this,' said Horace. 'Someone's bound to find us.'

Echo swallowed. She knew he was right. Here they were, stuck in the dark, in an enemy airship teeming with vicious pirates, heading for who knew where! When would they get back to the *Scarlet Margaret*? *Would* they get back to the *Scarlet Margaret*? She shook her head. There had to be a small chance that they'd make it.

She forced a smile on to her face and patted his arm. 'Stop worrying,' she said. 'We'll be fine. Do you still have the glow jar?'

Horace fumbled in his satchel and passed the jar over, shaking it gently to wake the little bugs inside.

Echo held it up, blinking in its light, and took in the barrels and crates around them. On the opposite side of the hold, a huge sheet of glass caught the light and Echo jerked back.

'What's that?' said Horace.

'I don't think you want to know,' said Echo, creeping closer. It was an enormous tank, twice as tall as Echo was, and it was full of water, but she couldn't make anything else out behind the dark glass. She peered so close her nose was almost touching it.

Gilbert emerged from her collar and sniffed at the tank too. 'I think it's empt—'

BANG!

A huge white snout loomed out and thudded into the glass

right in front of Echo's face. She shrieked and leaped backwards and the shape disappeared into the gloom with a flash of razor-sharp teeth and the flick of a huge, pointed dorsal fin.

'W . . . what was it?' Horace had arrived beside her.

Echo shoved him away. 'Shark,' she whispered.

'What? A real—'

'Yes.' Echo marched past him. There was no need to show Horace how scared she was. 'Let's hide.'

Echo was still shaking with terror as they crept back to their hiding place behind the SKY BISCUITS crate. She hugged herself tightly and stroked Gilbert's scales, which were white with shock. They would be just fine as long as they kept hidden, she told herself. After all, the shark was in a tank and they were out here. Just as long as they didn't get caught by Old Gus, that was.

There was a rumble of engines from the rear and *Obsidian* shuddered into life.

'We're off,' said Horace.

'But to where?' Echo replied. 'The Aqualiber Vaults, that pirate said. Have you ever heard of them?'

'No.'

'I suppose it doesn't matter *where* they are,' Echo said, with a shiver. 'Anywhere on land is better than being trapped in here.'

Horace nodded stiffly, but didn't say anything.

Echo took in his exhausted face. 'We should try to get a little sleep too, while we can. I'll take first watch.'

Horace settled himself behind a crate of gunpowder and lay down, his eyelids drooping. Gilbert curled comfortably round Echo's neck and closed his eyes too, but Echo kept herself propped up with her back to a barrel, the glow jar on her knees. She had to stay positive. With any luck, they'd moor somewhere near Sleepy Palms and she and Horace would be able to sneak out and find the *Scarlet Margaret*. They were due some good luck, weren't they?

The floor tilted and Echo felt *Obsidian* shudder and lift into the air. She glanced at Horace, who had already given in to sleep and was snoring softly. Guilt suddenly twisted in her stomach. He'd come to stay for a relaxing break and she'd put him in danger. Again. They were flying, but where to? And what would they do when they got there?

Echo's throat tightened. Why had she ever thought this would be a good idea?

CHAPTER THIRTEEN

'Echo, we're slowing down!'

Echo felt a tug at her sleeve and shook herself awake. For a moment, she'd forgotten where she was, then she took in the barrels and crates that filled the hold of *Obsidian* and the panic of the night before flooded back.

Horace's worried face peered down at her in the weak light of the glow jar. 'I think we must be here.' He looked around nervously. 'Wherever *here* is.'

Echo staggered to her feet and blinked the sleep from her eyes.

Gilbert shook himself and stretched on her shoulder.

The hold was eerily still without the rumble and roar of the engines at full power, and, every time the ship let out a creak, Horace jerked his head around in panic.

There was a *clank* and this time they both jumped as heavy boots rattled down a ladder. Horace quickly pocketed the glow jar and they shrank back behind the crates as lamps flickered into action and the hold was flooded with light.

'Where do you think we are?' whispered Horace.

'I don't know.'

'Let me see.' Horace stood up and squinted as the overhead lights lit up the hold.

Footsteps rang out on the metal floor and Gilbert froze on Echo's shoulders, his scales glowing scarlet for danger.

Echo shrank back behind a crate as a pirate came towards them. His dark hair was twisted into greasy spikes and he wore the shark-tooth collar of the Thunder Sharks round his throat, although his face was hidden in shadow. His heavy boots made the floor shake and his knuckles glinted with solid silver rings.

With a jolt, Echo realized Horace was still visible from where he stood, staring in horror at the pirate.

'Horace!' she hissed. She darted forward and grabbed his sleeve, pulling him back behind the crate.

'*No!*' Horace whispered. They both watched in horror as the glow jar flew out of his jerkin, as if in slow motion, and sailed through the air.

Echo's heart clenched as the jar spun away across the hold before disappearing from view. She could hear it still rolling across the riveted metal floor.

The rolling stopped.

The pirate's footsteps stopped.

There was a pause and then a gruff voice said, 'What's this?'

No! Echo's eyes widened in horror.

Gilbert's scales paled to white.

Horace put both hands over his face.

More footsteps came down the ladder. 'It's a glow jar,' said another voice, a woman's this time.

'But where's it come from, Mei?' The first voice sounded angry. 'There's someone in here.'

Horace gave Echo a stricken look. She glanced around, but there was nowhere for them to go.

Loud footsteps marched towards them. Echo cowered behind the crate as the two pairs of feet came closer. There was a crash and scuffling as crates and barrels were heaved aside.

'I know you're in there' yelled the man's voice. 'Better come out now, before we drag you out.'

Echo gripped Horace's hand.

Gilbert hid himself in her collar.

The footsteps came closer and Horace squealed as the crate they were hiding behind swung away with a gritty scrape.

The pirate's ferocious, stubbly face leered down at them.

'What do we have here?' His face twisted into a grin. 'Couple of kids!'

The second sky pirate, the one he'd called Mei, joined him. She was a big woman with swordfish tattoos up both arms and a head of black curls. 'You two are gonna regret this. Who're you with?'

Echo opened and closed her mouth. Should she tell them Lil was her mother? Would that scare them off? She took in the pirates' ferocious faces with a shiver. No, that might put them in even more danger. All the sky-pirate clans were rivals now the hunt was under way. She folded her arms and tried to look nonchalant. 'We're not with anyone.'

'How'd you get in 'ere?'

Echo shrugged.

Mei turned to Horace. 'You got a voice?'

Horace stared at the floor. 'We just needed a ride.'

Mei glared at them both, then turned to the first pirate. 'Check nothing's missing. I'll take 'em to Gus.'

Echo glanced at the closed gangplank, but there was nowhere to go and, before she had a chance to attempt to run for it, the woman pirate had grabbed her and was holding her cutlass to Echo's throat.

'No funny business,' Mei snarled. She looked at Horace. 'One wrong move and your friend gets it.'

The first pirate grabbed a coil of rope from one of the store piles and bound Horace's hands behind his back, before turning to Echo and doing the same.

'Move,' said Mei, prodding Echo between the shoulders with the tip of her blade.

Echo trudged up the ladder, blinking in the artificial light.

Throughout the ship, pirates hurried here and there, readying *Obsidian* for landing, only pausing briefly to stare at Echo and Horace as they were marched past.

They were ushered through a maze of narrow corridors with walls of hammered metal plates before finally arriving at a closed steel door. Furious shouting came from inside.

'Sounds like the boss is in a great mood,' said Mei, with a twisted smile.

As she pushed open the door, Echo saw Old Gus standing in the ship's cockpit with his back to them, waving his huge hands in fury.

'Well, grease 'im!' he bellowed. 'Do something. He goes down that vent by hook or by crook!'

The rest of the Thunder Sharks murmured among themselves and turned as they heard Mei approach with Echo and Horace.

Old Gus jerked round, the tails of his tatty blue furs flying.

'Something wrong, Cap'n?' asked Mei.

'Damn boy won't fit down the 'ole.' Old Gus waved a hand at a shivering Grub, who was being held by the ear by another ferocious-looking Thunder Shark. The pirate clutched a tape measure in his other hand. 'I knew we were being too generous with 'is rations.'

'We could starve 'im, sir?' suggested the pirate with the tape measure.

Grub let out a whimper and his chin trembled.

119

'We can't wait around for that!' Old Gus screamed, spittle flying through the air.

'B ... but, Cap'n. The others won't 'ave solved the clue as fast as yerself. They're not clever like you are.'

'Hmm ... I suppose that is true.' Old Gus stroked his bristly beard.

'And they won't even know about the vent,' chipped in another pirate, who stood trembling by the ship's wheel. 'They're not wise and knowledgeable like you.'

'All right, all right.' Old Gus seemed to have calmed down. 'Nothin' but water until 'e fits.' The pirate suddenly noticed Echo and Horace, who were cowering behind Mei. His eyebrows knitted together in rage again. 'What is the meanin' of this?'

'Found 'em in the hold, Cap'n,' Mei said. 'Hiding behind a crate. What should I do with 'em? Slit their throats first or feed 'em to Charlotte as they are?'

Old Gus considered them for a long moment. 'They're small,' he said eventually.

Mei looked confused. 'Well, they're children, boss. I'm sure they'll still taste all right. Charlotte's not exactly fussy.'

'No, no, don't feed 'em to her. They're just what we need, as it turns out,' said Old Gus. He looked at Echo and Horace in turn. 'Line 'em up next to 'im.' He pointed at a quivering Grub.

Mei shoved Echo and Horace over to stand by Grub. Echo

gave Horace a quizzical look, but he looked just as confused as she felt. What was going on?

Old Gus prowled up and down in front of them. 'They're small,' he said again. 'Perhaps small enough.' He gestured at the pirate with the tape measure. 'Size 'em up, Stanley.'

He turned to Echo. 'How'd yer like a chance to earn yer freedom?'

CHAPTER FOURTEEN

Echo looked at Horace, who was wide-eyed and frozen with fear, then turned back to Old Gus. 'W . . . what do you want us to do?'

Old Gus towered over them, the shark's-tooth collar round his neck glinting dangerously.

Gilbert trembled from where he was hidden down the collar of Echo's shirt.

'Now, listen up,' Old Gus said. 'I've got a job for one of you two. Do it right and you'll win yer freedom. Do it wrong and . . .' He drew his cutlass and mimed drawing it across his throat. 'Understand?'

Echo and Horace both gave shaky nods.

He sheathed the cutlass. 'We're lookin' for a map to . . .' He thought for a moment and cleared his throat. 'Doesn't matter where it's to. It's a map and we need it. We've worked out that it's hidden in the Aqualiber Vaults.'

'What are those?' Echo clapped her hand over her mouth as the words popped out without her meaning them to.

'Keep yer mouth shut,' snapped Old Gus, stepping forward menacingly. 'The Aqualiber Vaults are an underwater library containin' all the world's knowledge.' He pointed a black-stained finger at Horace. 'You are gonna go in there and bring the map back to me.' He glared at Echo. 'You'll stay here, as insurance.'

Echo stiffened, her fears forgotten for a moment. Why should *she* have to stay? She was the sky pirate – surely she should be doing the map-hunting? She folded her arms. 'I'd be much better at finding the map than him.'

Old Gus glared at her, then a smile twitched at his lips, although it didn't reach his eyes. 'Oh, would yer? You're gonna get it for me, are yer? A little girl?'

Echo bristled. How dare he? 'I'm not little.'

'We ... we could go together,' said Horace, his voice shaking. 'We'd find it quicker that way.'

'Oh no, no, no.' Old Gus shook his head, making his plaited beard swing back and forth. 'And how would I know you'd come back?'

'You'd have our word,' said Horace, sticking out his chin.

'Your word!' Old Gus let out a guffaw, but his eyes were fierce. 'Pull the other one, boy. No, one of yer goes and one stays here. Who's it gonna be?'

Echo shivered. Her plan to sneak out once they'd reached

land had gone horribly wrong. How were they ever going to find their way back to the *Scarlet Margaret* now the Thunder Sharks had them? She glanced at Horace for a moment and guilt flooded her as she took in his tired face. She needed to think of something. She'd got them into this mess, and she was supposed to be a sky pirate after all. The first step *had* to be to get away from the Thunder Sharks, and to do that they needed to find the map for Old Gus.

But what would Lil say if she heard that Echo had helped a rival crew? She frowned. She would just have to make sure she got a good look at the map, then she'd be able to help the Black Sky Wolves find the treasure first.

She set her jaw. 'I'll go,' she said.

'This is Aqualiber,' said Old Gus, pointing through the viewscreen as they drew closer to a coastal city of pale stone buildings built round a network of canals. He and Echo were standing by the ship's wheel, at the fore of the cockpit, Horace having been marched off to a cell by Mei. As Echo gazed out of the oval windows, she realized they were looking through the eyes of the shark-shaped ship.

As they flew over the city, she looked down and took in the labyrinth of waterways, bustling with tiny white rowing boats. Beyond the city limits were rolling hills peppered with clusters of dark pines. With a lurching stomach, she realized that there was no pale pink sand or shimmering turquoise water and not a single waving star-palm to be seen. They must have travelled even further away from Sleepy Palms. And from Lil.

Echo took a deep breath to steady herself.

'There's only one entrance to the Aqualiber Vaults – that blue door.' Old Gus pointed, passing his spyglass to Echo. She raised it to her eye. A flight of white marble steps led up from one canal to a huge, stone-columned building with an ornately carved door of brilliant blue lacquer.

'And you want me to go in there?'

'No.' Old Gus shook his head. 'It's only open to scholars and philosophers. There's no way any of us would get in. Besides, we don't want to draw attention to ourselves. Might give away the location to the others.'

'The others?'

Old Gus glared at her. 'That's no concern of yours.'

'So what do you want me to do?'

Old Gus pointed away from the city wharf, across the lagoon, to a tiny islet of purplish rocks. 'What do you see over there?'

'Nothing much.' Echo raised the spyglass to her eye again, but the islet was empty – a bare outcrop of craggy, lichen-crusted rock peeking through the waves.

'Keep lookin'.'

Echo stared through the spyglass until her eye watered, scrutinizing every centimetre.

'I still can't see anything,' she said.

'Watch the birds.'

'The birds?' Echo squinted through the lens as a flock of fluffy white cloud gulls sailed gracefully through the air. As they descended towards the rocks, a sudden gust of air blew them upwards and they whirled off, squawking in annoyance.

Echo passed the spyglass back to Old Gus. 'There's air coming out of the rocks,' she said.

Old Gus nodded with a twisted smile. 'The library's ventilation system. Keepin' all those books at the perfect level of humidity takes a lot of air. And that's where it goes in and out.'

Echo nodded slowly. So this was why Old Gus needed her. He wanted her to go down the vent! Images of dark, dripping tunnels filled her head and she shivered. 'Won't it be dangerous?' she said.

Old Gus snorted. 'I'm not yer mother. You'll do what yer told.'

'But why don't you send one of your crew down?' asked Echo. 'Wouldn't they be more reliable than a couple of kids?'

'We're all too big to fit down the vent. Even Grub. But you on the other hand ...' Old Gus looked at Echo. 'You'll do nicely. And I know you'll be reliable because otherwise yer friend ...' He drew one finger across his throat again with a grimace.

Gaping jaws with rows of razor-sharp teeth filled her head

and Echo's heart clenched at the thought of Horace being dropped into the murky water of the shark tank. Did she have a choice? No, she didn't. She finally shook her head in resignation. 'I'll try.'

'There's no try about it. Bring the map back or yer friend is shark food.' He handed her the piece of parchment with the riddle Rashmi the Ruthless had read out in the meeting.

Echo scanned it in despair. 'But you've only solved the first part. What if I can't work out the rest of the clue?' Her voice trembled and she had to fight to hold back tears.

'I have faith in yer,' growled Old Gus. 'Fear is a powerful motivator, I find. You've got until noon. That's four bells from now. Now, let's go.'

Old Gus stationed himself at the control deck and steered *Obsidian* towards the little island. As they reached it, the airship slowed to a hover.

'Hold 'er here,' said Old Gus to one of his crew. 'You, follow me.'

He took Echo down another corridor on the port side of the airship until they came to a closed hatchway. Old Gus pushed a button to the side of the hatch with one chunky black-nailed forefinger. The door hissed open with a clunk, letting a brisk sea breeze hit Echo full in the face. Old Gus unfurled a length of rope ladder and flung it out of the doorway. 'Down yer go,' he said.

'Fine.' Echo clenched her fists to steady herself. She'd get into the library, find the stupid map and get straight back out again. Horace would be fine and they'd be on their way back to the *Scarlet Margaret* in no time. She took a deep breath. She would keep telling herself this, however unlikely it might seem, or she'd never hold her nerve. Echo turned her back to the doorway, grabbed the rough rope in both hands and made her way down the swaying ladder.

Echo landed on the rocks, followed by Old Gus and Mei. She looked around. This place was nothing like the lazy warmth of Sleepy Palms or the icy blizzard at Shark's Fin Peak. Instead, the air was cool and fresh, filled with the scent of pine trees. Over on the mainland, Echo could see the city of Aqualiber, with its grand waterfront houses of pale stone and the labyrinth of canals winding between them.

'Come on, no time for sightseein'.' Old Gus prodded Echo between the shoulder blades with his sword.

Mei strode past them and went over to the air vent. She knelt down and prised off the grille with her cutlass. There was a metallic *ping* and one of the bolts flew into the air. Old Gus joined her and they worked quickly, loosening the metal grid until finally they pulled it free to reveal a narrow, sloping tunnel.

Echo peered into the ventilation shaft. A gust of warm, musty air pushed her back and she wrinkled her nose.

Old Gus and Mei fastened one end of a rope ladder to the edge of the opening where the grille had been attached and Mei gave it a hearty tug. 'Seems to hold, Cap'n,' she said.

Old Gus nodded and threw the rest of the ladder into the shaft. Echo heard it slithering open and bouncing down the walls. After a few moments, there was a distant thud as the end hit the bottom far below. Just how deep was this tunnel? And what was waiting for her at the bottom? Did Old Gus even know?

'Get down there,' said Old Gus, with a sneer.

Echo took a last quick look around, then spat on both hands, rubbed them together and clambered backwards down the ladder and into the darkness.

As she descended into the warm murk, she heard Old Gus cry after her, 'Noon, remember! We'll be waitin'!'

As if she could forget. Echo tried to push her worries about Horace out of her mind as she squeezed her way down. The ventilation shaft was indeed too narrow for adults to have fitted through, and it was hard work inching her way down the rope ladder, banging elbows and knees on the metallic sides of the shaft and catching her clothing on the rivets that held the sections together.

She glanced down into the gloom, but couldn't make anything out. Who knew how deep this ventilation duct even went? If she lost her grip for a moment and fell . . . Echo shook herself. No, she wouldn't think about that. She couldn't fall at the first hurdle. She had to get into the library, solve the rest of the clue and find that map. The sooner she did that, the sooner Horace would be safe, and the sooner they'd be back on the *Scarlet Margaret* with Lil and the crew.

Echo set her jaw and kept going.

By the time she'd reached the bottom of the shaft, Echo's hands were raw and so stiff she could barely grip the ropes any more. She collapsed on to the floor and looked around.

She had emerged into a large, dimly lit room with walls of thick blueish-purple glass bricks that bent the light into strange, rippling shadows. A series of huge fans whirred on the far wall, their blades slicing the air rhythmically and sending a steady wind whistling through the room.

'Where now?' said Echo aloud.

Gilbert crawled out of her jerkin pocket and blinked, then pointed his snout at the only exit – a corridor that curved away from them through the murky glass.

'Well, here we go,' said Echo, taking a deep breath and gathering all her courage. She'd been to libraries before, first in the castle at Lockfort (even though it had been out of bounds) and then in Port Tourbillon. But both those times she had been with Horace. *And nobody had been in deathly danger*, she thought grimly. She stroked Gilbert's scaly tail and made off down the glass-walled corridor.

When she got to the end, she gasped.

She was standing on an endlessly long balcony, high above

the library stacks. The roof of the building was made entirely of glass and above them Echo saw shoals of iridescent fish slide past. Of course, they were beneath the sea! She leaned over the balcony rails and took in the enormity of the library below. Stack after stack of shelves stretched out as far as she could see.

'How big is this place?' she murmured. 'It goes on forever!'

A prickle of fear ran down her spine. These vaults were huge. Even if she could solve the clue, how was she ever going to find the map in somewhere as large as this? And what would happen to Horace if she failed?

CHAPTER FIFTEEN

'Oh, Gilbert,' Echo said in dismay, as they looked over the balcony railing. 'It's hopeless.'

Below them, the library spread out like a never-ending labyrinth of bookshelves. Echo's head spun. How could she possibly find the map in all of this?

The little lizard curled his tail round her neck and nudged her cheek gently as if to say, *Keep your chin up – we can do it.*

Echo stroked his scales. He was right: they could do it. They had to. She took a deep breath and looked further along the balcony. A few metres away, the balustrade of a spiral staircase emerged from the floor.

'Come on,' she said. 'We'd better get started.'

The descent down the spiral stairs was dizzyingly long and, by the time they got to the bottom, Echo felt like they must have travelled to the centre of the earth. From down here, the glass ceiling was so far away the glowing fish looked like constellations in a night sky. The only clues they were underwater were the strange shadows that rippled over the floor from above.

Echo crept into the library's vast, shadowy chamber. The walls were covered in bookcases with gaps forming open archways leading to the different sections. The ventilation system blew a steady stream of salty air that stirred the ruffles on Echo's shirt and blew her curls across her eyes. At first glance, she thought the library floor was made of sand, but, when she looked more closely, she saw it was an intricate pattern of hexagonal tiles in shades of beige and gold that shimmered like the sandy seabed itself. The bookshelves looked as if they had been constructed from driftwood: greyish, weathered and worn smooth by the sea.

But there wasn't time to watch and wonder, she reminded herself. There were only a few short hours until Horace would be shark food! Echo went to the first shelf and ran her fingers along the spines of the books.

'I suppose this is as good a place to start as any,' she said.

Gilbert scuttled down her shoulder and began to inspect them too, cocking his conical eyes this way and that as he inched along the shelf.

Echo read title after title, hoping that one of them would give her a flash of inspiration or yield some kind of clue, but there was nothing about time or maps or the Cutlass of

Calinthe, or anything at all that might help her. She frowned and kept searching.

Gilbert gave a sudden chirp and Echo jerked her head up to see that he had frozen mid-step and turned danger red.

'What is it?' she hissed.

But Gilbert just bobbed his head as if to say, *Listen.*

Echo froze. Somewhere in the depths of the library, she could hear a rhythmic, squeaking sound. And it was getting louder.

As the squeaking got closer and faster, there was a sudden crash and Echo heard something rattle across the tiles like marbles.

'Ouch!' came a cross voice. 'Oh, so unfair. How did you get there? On shelves, you should be. Not on the floor to trip me and slip me. Oh my *beans*!'

There was a metallic scraping noise and another bang, and then the strange squeaking started up again.

Echo, who had been mesmerized by what she'd heard, hadn't even thought to hide. She glanced around in panic. Where was there for her to go? The room they were in didn't harbour any hiding places. The only option was back up the spiral staircase. She grabbed Gilbert, flung him over her shoulder and made for the archway.

'Can I help you?' croaked the voice behind them, just as Echo was about to throw herself through. She turned to see a most peculiar sight.

There, astride a shiny red tricycle, was a tiny, wizened old man wearing a charcoal velvet cloak. He took a crumpled paper bag from his pocket and offered it to Echo.

'Jelly bean?'

'Er ... thank you,' said Echo, reaching uncertainly and plucking out a shiny pink sweet.

'Would the little lizard like one too?' asked the man.

Gilbert bobbed his head and flicked his tongue out eagerly in response.

The man tossed a blue bean into the air and Gilbert caught it neatly in his mouth.

Echo shrugged and carefully put the sweet into her mouth

too, letting it melt creamily on her tongue. It tasted of strawberries and cinnamon. Her stomach rumbled.

'Gerund Rooksbill, chief librarian of the Aqualiber Vaults,' said the man, extending a tanned, crinkly hand. 'Just let me know what it is you're looking for and I'll point you in the right direction. I am duty-bound to assist anyone who is searching for information. Even if they appear to be –' he cleared his throat and looked her up and down – 'some kind of pirate.'

He puffed up his chest. 'Anyway, this isn't an ordinary library, you know? All the knowledge of the world is stored here. It could take you a lifetime to find what you need if you don't have the right guide.'

'Oh,' said Echo. She had to admit that Gerund was right. There were so many rooms, so many shelves, so many books. And they only had until noon! She glanced at Gilbert, who bobbed his head encouragingly. Yes, she would just have to trust this funny old man.

'I'm trying to solve a riddle,' she said.

Gerund wrinkled his nose. 'I'm afraid I'm not very good at those. Facts are more my forte. To help you get started, why don't we see what I've got on riddles? Follow me!'

Before Echo could answer, Gerund had jumped on to his tricycle and pedalled off at speed, cloak flying and wheels squeaking, leaving her staring, open-mouthed.

CHAPTER SIXTEEN

Echo raced after the librarian through the maze of rooms. Although he rode fast, and he often disappeared from view, she was able to keep up by following the sound of his squeaking wheels. Every so often, there'd be a crash and a shout of, 'Oh my beans!' and Echo would run round the latest corner to find him sprawled on the floor, his tricycle upside down, with its wheels spinning, and jelly beans strewn all around. But he would soon pick himself up and be off, with Echo yet again jogging to keep up.

Finally, when Echo thought she could run no more, they reached the centre of the library, where a clock tower stretched up into the heavens. The librarian stopped in front of a bank of wheels and dials.

Echo skidded to a halt behind him, nearly dislodging Gilbert from where he clung round her neck.

'Here we are,' said the librarian. 'Just a little reconfiguring to do.'

'Reconfiguring?' Echo frowned in confusion. Could she really trust him? The clock began to bong and she glanced up at the tower. It was already nearly nine bells in the morning. No time to lose!

Gerund took several cards punched with holes from a box and slotted them into the front of the machine, then turned the wheels. There was a grinding, clicking sound and, to Echo's astonishment, the bookshelves all around them revolved on their axes and reconfigured themselves.

'That should do it,' said Gerund. 'Here we have riddles, puzzles and paradoxes.' He gestured to the next room and Echo followed him inside.

Echo, Gerund and Gilbert searched the shelves for what seemed like hours, but no matter how many books they scoured they found nothing that would help Echo solve the riddle.

'Tell me more about this riddle,' said Gerund, popping a jelly bean into his mouth.

'Here.' Echo handed him the parchment that Old Gus had given her.

'*To find the way to dragon caves, seek knowledge underneath the waves,*' read Gerund.

'Knowledge underneath the waves is the Aqualiber Vaults,' said Echo. 'Old Gus worked out that part.'

'Next it says: *for seventy rungs you'll need to climb, if you're to find the map in time.*'

'But where are the rungs? And I know we're running out of time, but how does that help—'

BONG! At that moment, the clock above rang the hour again, drowning out Echo's words. She glanced anxiously up at it. Ten bells. Only two hours until Horace was shark food!

Gilbert suddenly gave an excited chirrup and raced up the bookshelf, right to the top. He pointed his tail at the clock.

'I know, Gilbert. I'm going as fast as I can!' Echo snapped, then crumpled in despair. 'Oh, it's impossible. Horace is going to die a gruesome Thunder Shark death and my mother will never find me and I'll be lost for ever under the sea with nothing to eat but jelly beans and it's all *my* fault!'

Gerund's face fell and Echo flushed with guilt. 'I'm sorry,' she said quietly. 'The jelly beans were very nice really.'

There was an awkward silence, then Gilbert raced down the shelves, grabbed her sleeve in his mouth and tugged at it.

'*What?*'

He pointed his tail at the clock again.

'Yes, I can see it's ten bells already. You're not helping!'

Gilbert shook his scaly head in exasperation and jabbed his tail at the clock for a third time.

'What do you ... Oh! Wait, that's it!' Echo said. 'You're right!' She picked him up and planted a kiss on his snout, making his scales turn pink.

Gerund stared at her and cocked his head inquisitively. 'Have you solved it?'

'Time!' she said. 'If you're to find the map *in time*. It's been staring us in the face all along.' She jumped up. 'It's not in a book at all. It's in the clock.' She turned to him. 'How do I get up there? Is there a stairway?'

'A ladder.'

'With seventy rungs?' Echo's heart skipped.

'Yes,' said Gerund. 'But you don't really mean you're going to—'

'Yes. Just tell me how to get up there.'

'But I couldn't possibly allow it,' said Gerund. 'It's completely unheard of.'

'Gerund,' said Echo, thinking quickly, 'there is information inside that clock. Are you telling me you're going to withhold that from me? Isn't that against the rules? Isn't it your duty to help me?'

'No, no, I don't mean ...' Gerund twisted his hands nervously. 'Of course I must help you, if that's what you want. It's just ... are you sure?'

'Positive,' said Echo. 'Come on – we don't have much time!'

'I haven't had cause to use the ladder for many a year. I don't know what shape it'll be in,' said Gerund.

'It doesn't matter,' said Echo. 'I have to get up there. Now, are you going to help me find my information or not?'

Gerund pulled open the door to the clock tower with a creak

and revealed the ladder inside – a tall and rickety affair, held together with what looked like string and sticky tape.

Echo put her head through the doorway and peered upwards, where the long pendulum swung back and forth inside the body of the clock. Gilbert sprang on to the ladder rail and shimmied up into the darkness. Echo took a deep breath, slung her satchel over her shoulder and followed him.

Gilbert, whose sticky toes gave him a natural advantage, made much quicker work of the climb than Echo did. When he reached the top, he turned and looked back at her with an encouraging chirrup.

'Coming!' Echo's arms and thighs were burning with the effort, and the ladder creaked and wobbled ominously, but she gritted her teeth and continued ever upwards. Risking a glance back down, Echo immediately regretted it as her head swam at the sight of the distance she'd climbed. She closed her eyes and gripped the rungs with all her might.

There was another chirrup from above her. She squinted up to see Gilbert navigating his way back down to her, head first.

'I'm okay,' she muttered, as Gilbert crept up her arm and gently prodded her cheek with his snout. 'Just a little further.'

She took a deep breath and started to climb again, one sweaty hand over the other, until she finally dragged her body over the top rung and lay panting on the blissfully horizontal wooden ledge behind the clock face. Up close, the tick and tock was so loud it seem to reverberate through Echo's bones.

Gilbert cocked an enquiring eye at her as she pushed open a little door and crawled out to the bracket beneath the clock face.

'How do we open it, Gilbert?' Echo knelt up and pulled at the rim, but it didn't budge. Could the map really be inside? Perhaps this wasn't the answer after all.

Gilbert ran up her arm and peered at the clock too, then shook his head and curled his tail into a question mark. He leaped lightly on to the minute hand of the clock. As the hand crept up to twelve and began its descent again, Gilbert's weight forced it forward with a clicking sound.

'That's it!' Echo tickled the little lizard under the chin. That was the final part of the clue.

*Face up to me and hold my hand. A trio and
quarter's the place to land.*

She grinned and gently turned the hour hand to three. There was a gentle grinding of machinery from inside as something slipped into place. 'That's the trio, now for the quarter.' She scooped Gilbert off the minute hand and turned it to three as well.

Echo held her breath as, with a *click*, the clock face swung silently open.

Inside was a dark chamber. Echo peered in, but she couldn't see anything. If only she still had the glow jar! She reached in blindly, half expecting to find spiders' webs, or worse, but the inside of the cavity was cool and as smooth as glass under a fine layer of dust. Emboldened, Echo reached in further until finally her fingers closed over something wrapped in paper. But what was it? It was no map, that was for sure. She pulled the little package out. It fitted comfortably in the palm of her hand and was solid and weighty.

She swung the clock face closed and sat on the ledge to examine what she'd found. It was wrapped in crumpled brown parchment and tied with string. Gilbert jumped lightly on to her shoulder and cocked an enquiring eye as she fumbled to untie the knots.

But, when she finally peeled off the parchment wrapper, her heart sank with disappointment. It wasn't a map at all, but an old silver pocket watch, mottled and tarnished with age.

'This isn't a map,' she said, her voice almost breaking into sobs as she glanced at the clock face again. Only half a bell till noon! 'Oh, what are we going to do?'

Gilbert ran down her arm and raced over to the discarded parchment. He grabbed it between his jaws and dragged it back.

'What are you doing? That's just the . . . Oh!' Echo scrubbed her tears away with her sleeve and picked up Gilbert and the parchment in delight as she saw the outlines, faded outlines, but outlines all the same, on the inside of the paper.

'*This* is the map. Gilbert, we've found it!'

CHAPTER SEVENTEEN

The clock gave a loud *bong* that startled Echo so much she almost toppled off the ledge she was balancing on.

'Young lady, please hurry!' Gerund called from far below on the library floor. 'It'll be high tide at any moment.'

High tide? Echo still didn't know quite what the librarian meant, or why it was so important, but she could hear the worry in his voice. Whatever it was, it was urgent, and she had a deadline to meet too.

'Coming!' she yelled. She shoved the parchment and the pocket watch into her knapsack, put out an arm for Gilbert to leap on to and made her way back down the rickety ladder, half climbing and half slithering to the library floor.

As she jumped down from the last rung, she found herself splashing into a puddle.

'Oh mercy me! The stacks! The stacks!' The librarian leaped on to his tricycle and pedalled off through the water to the bank of wheels. He began spinning them frantically. As he did so, the bookshelves revolved on their axes again and disappeared into the ground, and only just in time, as foamy waves of clear seawater came surging across the library floor.

'Quick, to the exit!' he panted, as the final shelf clanked into position and Echo found herself in the centre of a vast, open, shelfless library. The librarian pedalled away with Echo splashing after him, Gilbert clinging on tightly to her shirtsleeve.

The water was soon ankle-deep and perfectly clear, with just the odd piece of seaweed or crab or stray book floating on its surface.

As the water reached Echo's knees, it became harder and harder to run or even walk. Even the librarian had to stop his tricycle. But the exit still seemed miles away across the huge atrium.

'How high does the water get?' panted Echo.

'Right to the top,' said Gerund. 'You'll have to jump on the back.'

Echo stared for a moment at the little red tricycle, then shook her head in disbelief and got on.

He pulled a cord on the tricycle's framework and, with a *whoosh,* three balloons inflated round the wheels and Echo let out a yelp as the little tricycle, or hovercraft, or whatever it was, bobbed up on to the surface of the water.

'Right, let's get you to the exit,' said the librarian. 'Usually, I have visitors out before high tide. This is all completely against protocol.' He made to pedal towards the far end of the hall, away from the ventilation shaft.

'Er, I came in that way,' said Echo, pointing back towards the stairway.

'I see.' Gerund raised one white eyebrow and spun the tricycle round.

There was a deafening roar from behind them.

'Hold on!' shouted the librarian. 'Sounds like a big 'un!'

Echo gripped his waist and turned to see a huge, white-crested wave, as tall as a house, surging towards them. She squeezed her eyes shut and held on tight as they were thrown forward, water slapping them, foam soaking her clothes and plastering her hair to her head. She held her breath as they were buffeted about, but then the wave carried them forward at an alarming pace.

Echo spat out seawater and dragged the hair from her eyes to see the long, gilt-railed balcony, now at sea level, up ahead.

With one final burst of speed, the librarian pedalled the tricycle forward and landed on the balcony.

'You'll need to hurry,' he said, dismounting. 'But I've got something for you before you go.' He reached into his gown and drew out a small blue rectangle. 'Your library card. Should you ever need the services of the Aqualiber Vaults, you are now a member.'

'Thank you!' Echo took the card and carefully stowed it in her knapsack.

'And some jelly beans, for the journey,' said Gerund. 'I find them very useful on adventures.'

Echo grinned. Then another roar of surging water sounded. 'Now, hurry!' said the librarian.

Echo shoved the jelly beans into her knapsack and raced off up the balcony towards the ventilation shaft.

'Bye,' she yelled over her shoulder, 'and thank you again!'

Echo climbed back up through the ventilation shaft as quickly as she could, trying to outrun the waters that were rising below her. Finally, just when she thought she could climb no more, she reached the top and emerged blinking into daylight and fresh sea air.

She hauled herself out and collapsed, panting, on the rocks by the feet of a startled Thunder Shark, whom she identified as Stanley. Water streamed from her hair and clothes and Gilbert climbed out of her pocket, shaking droplets from his scales.

'She's back!' he exclaimed. 'Oi, boss, she's back!' He turned to Echo. 'You got it? You better 'ad.'

'She is?' Old Gus's eyebrows shot up in astonishment, but his familiar glare soon returned. 'You're late,' he snarled, storming across the rocks towards Echo. 'Hand it over.'

A flicker of fear ran through her as she unfastened the straps of her soaking knapsack. Would all that water have ruined the map? But, as she reached inside, she realized that, by some miracle, the paper was only damp. She paused as she smoothed out the crumpled parchment, trying to take in every detail of the spidery outlines, but she didn't recognize any of the names, and the coastlines were unfamiliar too. She couldn't just hand it over to Old Gus, not just like that. She should be taking it to Lil! Then the Black Sky Wolves could find the treasure. But, she realized with a sinking heart, she had no choice. If she didn't give it to Old Gus, Horace would die a horrible death. Guilt weighed heavily in her stomach. No, she would have to give it up. But somehow she couldn't quite bring herself to do it.

Before she had a chance to ponder any further, Old Gus snatched the parchment from her hand. He studied the map. 'Tarakona Canyon, eh?' he muttered to himself. 'Right in the heart of the Dragonlands. I shoulda known!' He shoved the parchment into his jerkin and clapped his large hands together, a mad glint in his eye. 'Right, lads and lasses!' he bellowed. 'Full steam ahead to Tarakona Canyon. The race is on!'

He turned on his heel and marched back to the ship, the other sky pirates hurrying after him.

'Hey, wait a minute!' shouted Echo. 'Haven't you forgotten something?'

Old Gus waved his hand at her without looking back. 'Yes, yes, you're free to go.'

'But what about Horace?'

'Horace?'

'My friend. You said if I brought you the map, you'd let him go.'

'Ah, we've had a slight change of plan.' Old Gus chuckled cruelly. 'Turns out young Horace is a useful crew member. Good at readin'. We'll be keepin' 'im.'

Keeping him? Echo felt dizzy. How could she have been so stupid? She'd trusted a pirate, and the leader of the dreaded Thunder Sharks at that! She felt sick. She should have known he wouldn't keep his word.

'But you can't! You promised!' she shouted.

'I think yer'll find I can do whatever I like.'

Echo's shock turned to rage and she whipped *Stinger* from her boot, brandishing it at him with one shaking hand. 'I won't let you take him.'

Old Gus smiled a horrible smile. 'Really?'

'I'll fight you.' Echo shook the little sword at him again.

'Oh, will yer?' In one swift movement, Old Gus whipped his cutlass from its scabbard and flicked *Stinger* out of Echo's hand. It arced through the air and landed on the rocks with a *clang*. Echo stumbled sideways, lost her balance and fell backwards, skinning both palms and landing on her bottom with a thud.

Old Gus marched off, laughing, towards *Obsidian*. 'Fire up the engines, lads!' he yelled over his shoulder as he stomped up the gangplank.

'You can't take him!' Echo shouted after him, but he didn't

turn round and neither did any of the other Thunder Sharks, who were racing here and there, frantically readying *Obsidian* for take-off.

Echo was still sprawled on the rocks, sobbing, when the engines roared and the Thunder Sharks surged into the air in a cloud of foul-smelling smoke. Off they soared, far into the distance, taking the map, and Horace, with them.

CHAPTER EIGHTEEN

Echo watched helplessly as *Obsidian* got smaller and smaller, until finally the ship shrank to a dot on the horizon and disappeared. Panic washed over her as she glanced round the deserted island. Stranded! And what would happen to Horace? Things were getting worse and worse. He might be safe from the shark tank, for the moment, but how would she ever get him back?

'Oh, what are we going to do?' she wailed.

Gilbert clambered up on to her shoulder and touched her cheek gently with his snout in a way that said, *Don't worry – we'll figure something out.*

'I guess we will,' she said, smiling weakly and tickling his crest. But inside Echo had no idea how she'd manage it. There was no way off the island. Across the waves, she could see the stone buildings of Aqualiber, but, even though Bulkhead had taught her to swim in the last few weeks at Sleepy Palms, she knew it was much too far for her to manage. The ventilation shaft that led back into the library was still full of gurgling water, so that route was out too.

Echo sighed and sat down on the rocks, her head in her hands. She was trapped, at least until the tide went out.

She felt a nudge to her shoulder and looked up to find Gilbert flashing his crest.

'What is it?' she said.

She followed the little lizard's gaze to see a small black shape on the horizon. She squinted at it. Another airship. Of course! The other sky-pirate clans must have worked out the clue by now. Her heart lifted for a moment. Could it be the *Scarlet Margaret*? Had Lil solved the first part of the clue too?

Echo continued to watch as the airship approached. But, as it got closer, she realized with a sinking heart that it wasn't the *Scarlet Margaret* at all. It was another ship – smaller and sleeker with a green-silk balloon and, at its prow, a flag with a skull and crossbones entwined with snakes.

Echo wracked her brains. Which of the sky-pirate factions had the snake emblem? The Scurvy Sea Snakes – that was it! She watched as the ship approached the entrance to the Aqualiber Vaults, several hundred metres away across the water. She heard its engines hum as it slowed to a hover, before flying over to the harbour and weighing anchor near the sailing boats.

After a few moments, a hatch on the side of the ship popped

open and a metal gangplank slithered out. Echo stared as the flame-haired figure of Miranda Vossberg stepped out. She wore high-heeled green boots, dark breeches, a frilly white shirt and an emerald cape that billowed in the salty air. Echo squinted in the midday sun. There was a brilliant-green something round Vossberg's neck as well, a scarf perhaps, although Echo couldn't make it out exactly.

Echo reached for her knapsack and drew out Horace's spyglass. When she focused in on Vossberg, she drew back in surprise. The scarf wasn't a scarf, but a vivid green snake, its head swaying from left to right and its tongue aflicker. Vossberg strode over to the blue-lacquered library entrance and Echo saw her rap sharply on it with her knuckles. But Echo knew there would be no answer. Where did Gerund even go at high tide?

After waiting for a few minutes, Vossberg stamped her foot impatiently. Echo saw her take her own spyglass from the pocket of her breeches and scan round the bay. Too late, she realized Vossberg was going to see her and, for one brief moment, they were staring down their spyglasses at each other.

Echo gasped and dropped the spyglass. It fell with a *clang* and rolled along the rocks. Echo glanced around for somewhere to hide, but there was nowhere. She dropped to the ground, trying to make herself as small as possible.

When she looked up, Vossberg was still looking through the spyglass across the water, staring straight at her.

Echo watched as Miranda Vossberg disappeared back into her ship. There was a distant *click click click* as the gangplank coiled up and a *hiss-clunk* as the hatch closed behind it. Echo heard the engines fire and tried to hold down the fear that swelled in her stomach as the ship turned its nose towards her and approached the little island. Not another sky-pirate clan to deal with! What if the Scurvy Sea Snakes were even worse than the Thunder Sharks?

Gilbert nudged her shoulder.

'Perhaps she'll help us,' Echo said, her voice wobbling. 'She's part of the Seven Skies Alliance after all.'

Gilbert bobbed his head, but his scales were pale and, as the ship weighed anchor and the hatch hissed open, he scrambled into her knapsack and hid.

As Miranda Vossberg stalked towards her, Echo pushed her shoulders back and tried to make herself as tall and sky-piratey as she could be, although she couldn't quite manage to stop her legs from trembling.

Miranda stopped in front of Echo and smiled. 'And what have we here?' she said, putting her hands on her hips. She tapped one green-nailed finger on her chin. 'A girl, all alone on an island. But how did you get to the island? *Are* you alone?'

Echo dipped her head and said nothing. She probably couldn't trust this Vossberg woman any more than she could trust Old Gus. But what other choice did she have?

She looked up to find Vossberg regarding her, a faint smile

still on her pink-glossed lips. The snake round her neck flicked its tongue at Echo.

Miranda reached into her cloak and pulled out a green velvet pouch, retrieved a little white sweet and put it in her mouth.

The sweet smell of peppermint drifted towards Echo and her mouth watered.

Miranda arched one elegant eyebrow. 'Hungry?' She offered the bag to Echo.

Echo licked her lips, suddenly realizing she hadn't eaten anything but a few jelly beans for almost a whole day. One sweet wouldn't hurt, would it? After all, Miranda had eaten one.

'Thanks,' she said, her voice coming out in a croak. She took one of the smooth white pebbles and put it on her tongue.

'So, what happened?' asked Miranda, casually tossing a mint to her snake, which caught it with one deft snap of its jaws.

'They ... they left me here,' said Echo, sucking her mint. The sweet, sugary pastille made her bones flood with warmth and her tongue suddenly feel looser. She knew she shouldn't tell Miranda too much, but how else could she explain it?

'Who did?'

'The Thunder Sharks'

'*You're* a Thunder Shark? Gosh, I shall have to be careful!' Miranda pressed her green lacquered nails to her lips and her eyes sparkled with laughter.

'No!' Echo felt her cheeks burning.

'Good! I'm glad to hear it.' Miranda leaned forward and whispered theatrically, 'Don't tell anyone, but *I* think the Thunder Sharks are a bunch of brutes! Imagine! Dumping you here, just a little girl.' She reached forward and stroked a lock of Echo's hair.

Echo shrank back. 'I'm not a little girl, I'm a sky pirate!'

'But you said you weren't a Thunder Shark?' A frown creased Miranda's brow.

'I'm a Black Sky Wolf!' The words spilled from Echo's lips before she could stop them.

Miranda's eyes became sharp with recognition. 'Don't tell me. You're Lil's girl.'

'No, I . . .'

'Don't lie to me.' Miranda nodded slowly, as she looked Echo up and down. 'I can see it now. You look just like her.'

Echo swallowed, torn between cursing herself for giving so much away and feeling proud that she looked so much like her mother.

Miranda recovered herself and smiled again. 'So what are you doing out here, young Black Sky Wolf? Having adventures?'

Echo looked into Miranda's brilliant green eyes, still unsure whether she should trust her. But what choice did she have? If she wanted to rescue Horace, she was just going to have to persuade Miranda to help. She seemed friendly after all. Echo swallowed the rest of the peppermint and began to explain.

After Echo had told the whole story, Miranda appraised her for a moment.

'But you don't have this map?'

Echo shook her head. 'No.'

'Any idea where they were going?'

Echo bit her lip. 'If I tell you, will you help me get my friend back?'

Miranda folded her arms. 'You're hardly in a position to bargain. What if I leave you here? What are you going to do?'

Echo folded her arms. 'And what are you going to do without the map?'

Miranda nodded slowly. 'Okay, here's how it'll work. You help me find the dragon's lair. Once I have the Cutlass of Calinthe safely in my possession, I'll get your friend back.'

CHAPTER NINETEEN

Echo followed Miranda Vossberg up the gangplank and into *Anaconda*, the airship of the Scurvy Sea Snakes. *Anaconda* was a long, slim ship, made of gleaming silver plates that overlapped like the scales of a snake. Inside, it was eerily quiet, and Miranda's spike-heeled boots rang out as she strode through the corridor in front of Echo.

Something felt wrong, but Echo couldn't quite put her finger on it. As she followed Miranda past endless doors – to the armoury, the galley, the pristine, pod-like cabins – it suddenly occurred to her. Where was everyone?

'Where's your crew?' she asked.

'No need for a crew,' replied Miranda, over her shoulder. '*Anaconda* is fully automated.'

Echo peered into the galley as they passed. Inside, machines hummed and whirred under cold white light. It was a world away from the buzz and chatter of the *Scarlet Margaret*'s kitchens, where Spud and Skillet clanged ladles and pans, and cooked up spicy stews from the strangest of ingredients.

Echo hugged herself. 'Don't you get lonely with nobody else around?'

Miranda let out a delicate peal of laughter. 'Lonely? Not at all. I have Sylvester here.' She gestured to the snake draped round her shoulders, who eyed Echo curiously.

'I have a lizard!' said Echo, pulling Gilbert out from his hiding place in her knapsack and putting him on her own shoulder. He sniffed cautiously at Sylvester, then dived into Echo's collar as the snake's head darted forward, jaws wide.

'Sylvester!' Miranda slapped the green snake sharply on the snout and he recoiled. 'Where are your manners? You know you don't eat our guests.'

She unwrapped the snake from her neck and slipped him into a tank on the far wall of the cockpit, before striding over to the map cabinet.

'Now,' she said, turning to Echo, 'time for your part of the bargain. What exactly did this map look like? Do you remember any landmarks that showed where Tarakona Canyon might be?'

Echo bit her lip, still feeling disloyal for giving away all this information to another pirate captain, when she should be telling Lil. But she couldn't leave Horace with the Thunder Sharks. And she had to somehow get home to the *Scarlet Margaret*.

'It was just an ordinary map. The X was on Tarakona Canyon,' she said. She thought back to Old Gus's reaction. 'In the very heart of the Dragonlands.'

'But there must have been more than that!' Miranda snapped. 'Simply saying Tarakona Canyon isn't enough to find the lair. Wasn't there any other clue?'

'N . . . no,' said Echo, scrunching up her forehead and trying to recall something – anything – about the map.

Miranda shook her head in irritation, then gave a stiff smile. 'Well, I suppose we shall just have to go to the Dragonlands and see,' she said.

After poring over several sky charts, Miranda went to the cockpit and typed coordinates into the voyage computer.

'So what are the Dragonlands like?' asked Echo, taking a look at the charts herself. 'Are they far from here?'

Miranda's head jerked up, as if she'd forgotten Echo was there.

'It's a volcanic region to the far east of here,' she said finally. 'Dragons often nest inside volcanoes. They like the heat, you see. Creatures forged in fire like to stay close to it.'

'Forged in fire?'

'The eggs hatch in the heat of their mother's fiery breath,' said Miranda. She tapped her fingers on the dashboard. 'Now, our best bet is to aim for the Dragonlands, track down Old

Gus and follow him. Or, even better, intercept him and get that map. We'll stop at Amaranth Point and see if we can find out any more there.'

Echo studied the sky chart and saw Amaranth Point marked on the edge of the Dragonlands, over the Nordland Channel. 'What's at Amaranth Point?'

'It's the last trading post before the Dragonlands,' said Miranda. 'We'll stop there for supplies and ask around about this Tarakona Canyon. There's a chance Old Gus will stop off there too and if he does . . .' A grin spread across her face as she pulled on a lever and *Anaconda* lifted smoothly into the air.

'But what supplies will we—'

'So many questions!' said Miranda, with a stiff laugh. 'Aren't you hungry? Why don't you get something to eat from the galley?'

Echo licked her lips. She was famished, but she didn't want to leave Miranda alone. Not when there was so much she needed to know. 'I'm not hungry,' she lied.

'No, really, I think you are. Please go.' Miranda's voice took on a steely edge and a flicker of uncertainty ran down Echo's spine.

'Okay, I mean thank you,' said Echo. 'I was just wondering if I could send a message to my mother though. Do you have any postal pigeons?'

'I'll see to it,' said Miranda, without looking up. 'And you should get some rest too. Sleep in any cabin you like.'

'I don't feel tired.'

'I insist!' Miranda looked up sharply, then smiled. 'Children need naps, and you said you'd been up all night.'

'But what about sending the postal pigeon?'

'The postal pigeon?'

'To my mother. How will you know where to send it?'

Miranda blinked for a moment. 'Oh, don't you worry about that. The postal pigeon will know where to go. I'll see to it while you catch up on some sleep.'

'Thank you,' said Echo, her heart filling with hope. Once Lil knew where she was, the *Scarlet Margaret* would catch up with them in no time.

Miranda smiled. 'Now, you look exhausted. Off you go!'

Echo wandered back down the gleaming corridor to the galley and pressed the entry button. The door slid smoothly open and she stepped inside. Where the *Scarlet Margaret*'s kitchen was a merry mess of colourful vegetables and clattering pans, the galley of *Anaconda* was clinically white and silent. Every surface, from the shiny, handleless cabinets to the spotless metal worktops, was blank and smooth. In the central wall, a large machine whirred quietly.

Echo approached it. 'What do you think this does?' she said.

Gilbert emerged from where he'd been hiding in her shirt collar, glanced at the machine, sniffed it and curled his tail into a question mark.

The machine was covered in gleaming silver pipes, with

a central screen that said **Please make your selection**. Under the screen there was an empty cavity, and beside it a silver handle.

Echo turned the handle and, with a whirring of cogs, the letters flipped over and the writing on the screen changed.

Octo-Pie

'Octo-Pie? I'm not sure what that is, but I don't think I like the sound of it.'

Echo turned the handle again.

Peppermint pancakes

'I think I've had enough peppermints for now.' She tried again.

Cloud-cherry tart with almond custard

Gilbert bobbed up and down enthusiastically on her shoulder at this one. Echo's mouth watered. Perhaps Miranda was right. It did sound delicious.

'Now what?' She scanned the machine. There was only one button. 'Here goes.' She pressed it.

There was a whirring and clanking from inside the machine. Delicious, almond-scented steam wafted out. There was a *ding* and a small bowl full of cherry-soaked sponge clattered into

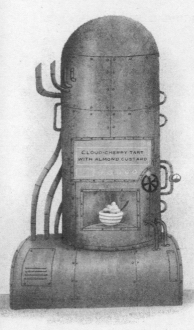

CLOUD-CHERRY TART
WITH ALMOND CUSTARD

the slot, followed by a thick stream of custard. Lastly, a silver spoon landed with a *plop* in the dish.

The whirring stopped and Echo carefully took the dish in both hands. She glanced around. There was nowhere to sit in the galley, so she went out into the corridor. At the far end, she glimpsed the cockpit where Miranda was still poring over her sky charts. Instead, Echo turned to the rear, where the crew capsules were. Unlike the *Scarlet Margaret*, with its cosy, wood-clad walls and swinging hammocks, *Anaconda*'s cabins were slick white pods with circular doors that opened with a *whoosh*. She peered into each one in turn. Each white, egg-shaped bed was freshly made, with shiny green silk sheets and plump yellow pillows. Echo picked the pod furthest to the rear and settled on the bed to eat the cake. She broke off a chunk for Gilbert and then dug in herself.

The whole ship swayed as *Anaconda* started to move.

Echo peered through the slit of a porthole. They were on their way to Amaranth Point, and the Dragonlands! She shivered. They must be getting further and further away from the *Scarlet Margaret*, and from Lil, but at least Miranda was sending the postal pigeon. Soon Lil would be on her way to find her. Longing swelled in Echo's stomach and she hugged herself. And she was a step closer to getting Horace back too. For now, all she could do was to make the best of things while she was here. She promised herself that she would learn as much as she could about the Dragonlands from Miranda, and about the Cutlass of Calinthe too.

And life onboard *Anaconda* didn't seem so bad. The food was delicious at least. There was no boring old deck-swabbing or patching of the mainsail to be done, and Miranda seemed perfectly friendly too. Maybe Echo could learn a few things about being a sky pirate from her while she was here.

She and Gilbert finished off their cake and Gilbert lapped up the last of the custard from Echo's bowl with his long tongue. Echo stifled a yawn. She was suddenly bone-tired from her almost sleepless night on the Thunder Sharks' ship, and Miranda's suggestion of a nap seemed like a good idea. She pulled off her boots and flung her knapsack on the end of the bed. It spilled open, shedding jelly beans all over the covers. Her spyglass and the pocket watch all tumbled out too.

Echo sighed and started to gather up the items. She put a jelly bean in her mouth and tossed one to Gilbert, then idly took the pocket watch in her hand. It read ten past eleven, but that wasn't right, as it was way past noon by now. It had obviously wound down. If only Echo had her clockwork tools with her! She turned it slowly in her hands.

'That's odd.' She frowned at the little clock. As she turned it to the left, the hands turned with her movement, so they were still pointing towards the bow of the ship. She turned it to the right, and the clock's hands turned again, continuing to point in the same direction.

Gilbert cocked one sleepy eye at the watch.

'There's something strange about this watch, Gilbert,' said Echo. 'I don't think this is supposed to tell the time at all.'

Gilbert sniffed it suspiciously.

Echo tilted it from side to side. Whichever way she turned it, the hands continued to point to the ship's bow. 'I think,' said Echo, excitement colouring her voice, 'it's a compass in disguise.'

But why would there have been a compass hidden with the map? Surely any sky pirate worth their salt would have one of their own? It was a puzzle.

Echo turned the compass over in her hands. The outer case was tarnished with age. She spat on her sleeve and rubbed at the casing.

'There's something engraved on here,' she said.

But Gilbert had fallen asleep on her pillow.

Echo pulled off her breeches and got into bed too, the pocket watch still clasped in her hand. But, despite her exhaustion, she couldn't sleep. The compass niggled at her – it was important somehow, she could feel it. She sat up and rubbed at it again with the corner of the bedspread. The tarnish was fading and an engraved picture was emerging. But of what? She held it up to the light and gasped. For carved in the silver was a dragon, breathing fire and perched on a mountain of treasure.

It's a clue, Echo thought to herself. *It's part of the map. And Old Gus doesn't have it!*

She clasped the compass to her chest. Old Gus might have a head start, but she had the second part of the map. If only she could work out what she was supposed to do with it.

CHAPTER TWENTY

Eventually, Echo drifted off into a deep sleep, waking early the next morning to find they'd left the warm climes of Aqualiber and were sailing above dense forests punctuated by brilliant blue lakes. She suddenly felt very far from home as she peered through the porthole. What would Lil be doing? Would she be looking for her? Would Miranda's postal pigeon even have reached her yet?

And how was poor Horace holding up? Echo shook her head. If only she could send a message to him too, to tell him that she was on her way, that she'd rescue him and everything would be all right. But it would put him in danger, even if Miranda did have another postal pigeon to spare.

She stretched and pulled on her boots. 'Come on, Gilbert,' she said, popping the little lizard on to her shoulder. 'We might not be able to contact Horace, but we can at least see where we are. Perhaps Miranda can show us the sky charts again.'

She went to the door, pushing the button so that it hissed open. Soft snores carried down the corridor from Miranda's cabin.

'I'm sure she won't mind if we take a quick look at the charts while we're waiting for her to wake up,' she whispered.

Gilbert gave a shrug of his scaly shoulders.

Echo tiptoed silently along the corridor until she came to the cockpit. *Anaconda* was still gliding along smoothly, and the control screen read **Autopilot**. Out of the viewscreen, Echo saw they were flying over the sea. Acres of murky grey water rippling with choppy white-tipped waves spread out before them.

Was this the Nordland Channel? Were they almost at the Dragonlands? Echo crouched down and slid open the first cabinet to find the chart. Inside were hundreds of scrolls of parchment, bottles of emerald ink and a long peacock-feather pen. She quickly riffled through the scrolls, but there were no sky charts to be seen. She slid the cabinet closed and moved on to the next one.

Inside were spyglasses, old goggles and a green leather aviator's cap. But still no charts. She moved on to the third and biggest cabinet. In this one was a heap of velvet sacks. Echo loosened the cord that gathered the neck of one and peeped inside to find an astonishing haul of sapphires as big as her fist. In another was a cluster of glittering diamonds. In yet another, handfuls of gold doubloons. Echo gaped at the wealth hidden in the cabinet.

Miranda was rich! She didn't even need to find treasure. There must have been enough jewels here to last her a lifetime.

Echo paused for a moment. Miranda wouldn't miss just one, would she? And wouldn't Lil be proud if Echo came back with jewels? They could use them for good – sell them to help the orphanage or buy food for the poor. She took a gleaming ruby in her hand, weighing it in her fist. But then she stopped. No, it wasn't right to steal, even if it was from another sky pirate. And especially when Miranda had been so kind to her. Echo wistfully put the ruby back in its pouch and slid the cabinet shut.

Echo turned to find Sylvester eyeing her suspiciously from his tank. Had he seen what she was doing? Echo shook herself. No, he was just a snake. And, even if he had, she hadn't been doing anything wrong. She forced herself to look brave and smiled. 'There's a good boy,' she said.

Sylvester hissed and lunged forward, his fangs flashing.

Echo jumped back in alarm.

There was a waft of peppermint, the click of heels on the metal floor behind her and Echo turned to see Miranda appear at the doorway. 'Up so early?' Miranda fixed Echo with her piercing green eyes. 'What were you doing in here?'

'I . . . I thought you'd be here. I wanted to see where we were.'

Miranda frowned and glanced round the cockpit, as if checking nothing was missing. She marched over to the voyage computer and pressed a button. A green map came up on the screen. 'We're just over the Nordland Channel and approaching Amaranth Point. You can see the Mallow Marshes up ahead.' She gestured through the viewscreen.

Echo squinted into the distance. On the horizon, she saw a glimpse of land beneath a murky pinkish haze.

'We'll have breakfast in Amaranth Point,' said Miranda, pulling a series of levers on the control panel. 'Let's get ready to descend.'

'Can I help?' asked Echo. 'I've flown an airship before.' She joined Miranda at the dashboard and examined the controls. Although a few of them were familiar to her from her voyages in Professor Daggerwing's *Hummerbird*, *Anaconda* had many, many more.

'What does this do?' she asked, pointing at a large, golden, triangular-shaped button.

'Oh, don't press that one!' said Miranda, with a laugh. 'That's how we lost poor Hana.'

Echo snatched her hand away. Who was poor Hana, and how had Miranda lost her?

Miranda must have noticed her perplexed frown because she giggled and pointed at the square outline on the cockpit floor. 'It's the control for the trapdoor. A useful exit if we ever need to get rid of . . .'

'Enemies?' offered Echo.

'Precisely.'

'Right.' Echo watched in unsettled silence as Miranda

expertly brought *Anaconda* down to land in the Mallow Marshes. As they got lower, Echo gazed out through the viewscreen across the rose-tinted landscape. They had reached the ground, but there were not many landmarks at all, just the woven reed walls that encircled the trading town of Amaranth Point, and a row of airships tethered outside in the sticky pink marshland. It seemed endless, swathed in mist and punctuated here and there by clumps of reeds or sludgy-looking islands with drooping trees. Through the fog, the faint golden glow showed the sun was coming up.

Miranda flicked a switch to slow the engines and they landed with a squelch next to the other ships.

'These are the Mallow Marshes,' said Miranda. She pressed a button and Echo heard a hatch open with a hiss. As the gangplank of *Anaconda* slid open, Echo breathed in the delicious scent of strawberries and vanilla. Gilbert's snout twitched greedily.

'What is that smell?' she said.

'That's the marshmallows,' said Miranda. 'They grow on the reeds here.' She pointed to a clump of tall, slender leaves.

'Marshmallows?' Echo gaped, then broke into a grin as she spotted the soft pink and white blobs growing on the tips of the reeds. Her mouth watered.

Miranda looked at Echo for a moment. 'Why don't you go and collect some while I get myself ready? Don't get lost though. You might come to a sticky end!'

'I'll be careful.' Echo slung her knapsack over her shoulder, rushed down the gangplank and waded out through the pinkish water to the nearest clump of mallow reeds.

Gilbert sprang from reed to reed, careful not to get his feet wet.

When they'd moved far enough away from *Anaconda*, and Miranda, Echo glanced around. Miranda was right. There really was nowhere to run away to, just endless pink marshland as far as the eye could see.

But wait, what was that? Something was moving on the horizon. Echo squinted into the early-morning sun, but it was too far away to make out.

'What is it?' she said. 'Can you see, Gilbert?'

Gilbert scuttled up to the top of the tallest reed and cocked one conical eye.

Echo grabbed Horace's spyglass from her bag and focused in on a strange, long-necked, woolly pink creature. As she watched, she realized it wasn't just one animal, but a whole herd of them. At first, they blended into the mallow rushes, but soon she could make out a whole pack of the peculiar beasts. And they were galloping straight towards her.

CHAPTER TWENTY-ONE

Echo stuffed the spyglass back in her bag, grabbed Gilbert and hurried back the way she had come. Behind her, she heard a peculiar braying noise. Then a splashing and sucking that grew louder as the herd of pink animals lolloped through the marsh towards them.

'Miranda!' Echo squelched as fast as she was able to back over to *Anaconda*, her knapsack bumping against her legs. 'Miranda, there's something—'

But, before she could get there, she was overtaken by the fluffy creatures, which barrelled past her, jostling her into the sticky pink water and sending her knapsack flying.

Echo put her hands over her head as she cowered among the reeds.

'What is it?' Miranda ran down the gangplank, her high heels ringing out on the shiny metal. Echo looked up to see her unholstering a flintlock pistol with an emerald grip.

BANG! Echo flinched as Miranda aimed and fired three shots over Echo's head.

Miranda's eyebrows knotted and her lips twisted into an ugly grimace. 'Missed.' She looked at Echo and broke into a smile. 'No need to be scared,' she said, popping a peppermint into her mouth. 'It's just a few overexcited marshmallamas.'

Echo got to her feet, looking around nervously, but the marshmallamas had disappeared into the mist. 'Are they dangerous?'

'No, not in the slightest.' Miranda holstered her pistol with a laugh and stepped off the gangplank. 'You should have stood still and they'd have run straight past you.'

Echo stopped and frowned. 'So why did you shoot at them?'

'Oh –' a smile curled on Miranda's lips – 'just sport.'

She pressed a fingertip to a sensor on the exterior of *Anaconda* and the doors shut behind her. There was a bleep, three green lights flashed and a robotic voice said, *Armed*.

'Come on,' she said. 'We've no time to waste. Let's go and get those supplies.'

Echo shook the pink water out of her hair and followed Miranda in silence to the town gate, an uneasy feeling settling in her stomach. It didn't seem very sporting to shoot at innocent creatures, if that's what the marshmallamas were. She shrugged. Miranda couldn't have meant to hit them – that was the only explanation.

Miranda rapped on the gate with her knuckles. After a few

moments, a hatch in the door slid open and a man's grimy face peered through the slot.

'Name?' he said.

'Miranda Vossberg.'

His eyes widened in shock. 'W ... welcome to Amaranth Point,' the man said. The hatch slammed shut, there was the noise of several bolts sliding back and the town gate swung open.

Amaranth Point was a higgledy-piggledy little town of wooden houses that teetered on stilts above the swampy waters. The buildings were connected by a slippery wooden boardwalk and every path seemed to lead to the central square, where an open-air market was in full swing.

Echo followed Miranda past stalls selling dried meats and dragon-defence talismans, dodging sword-swallowers, fire jugglers and a lady singing a song about a serpent who'd eaten her long-lost love. The air was full of the sweet scent of marshmallows, but also, less pleasingly, clouds of mosquitoes that buzzed round Echo's head.

'Right, let's get going.' Miranda consulted a list written in green ink on parchment and marched over to a stall marked **Verne's Adventurer's Outfitters**.

As Miranda read out her list to the man behind the stall, Echo glanced round the square. In a pen at its centre, a marshamallama trader paraded his flock of fluffy, braying beasts, while an auctioneer in a floppy pink hat bellowed out numbers through a megaphone to the eager crowd. Now that she was closer, Echo could see that the creatures *were* quite harmless. They were as tall as Miranda, but they seemed to be mostly neck and had gentle brown eyes with long lashes, and fluffy tails that wagged eagerly when the trader scratched them behind the ears.

'That will do nicely,' said Miranda, as Echo turned back. The man bagged up a huge black bullwhip, a large paper bag marked **MARSHMALLOWS** and a great many glow jars.

'We're heading to Tarakona Canyon,' Miranda said, as she opened her purse. 'I don't suppose you'd know the most efficient route?'

'Never heard of it,' said the man, with a shrug. 'And here are the flame-retardant gloves. In total, that's twenty doubloons.'

'If you could point me in the direction of someone who does know,' said Miranda, holding out a whole handful of gold coins, 'I'd make it worth your while.'

The man's eyes bulged. 'You'd better ask Cerise,' he said, reaching out to take the gold.

'Cerise?' Miranda's fingers closed over the coins.

'In the World's End.' He jerked his head towards a rickety-looking tavern on the edge of the square.

'I see.' Miranda closed her fist and pocketed the coins.

'Hey, you said ...'

'Twenty doubloons, wasn't it?' Miranda grabbed the bag of supplies, plucked out two tarnished coins, threw them at the man and turned on her heel, with Echo scuttling after her.

The World's End tavern was surprisingly clean and cosy, with a roaring fire and pink woollen cushions on every seat. Echo and Miranda settled themselves at a corner table.

They were soon eating a sweet but rather sickly breakfast of marshmallarmalade on toast, washed down with marshmallama milkshakes.

'I'm afraid there's not much else that grows around here,' said Miranda, with a smile. They both looked up as a barmaid with shocking pink hair piled up in a heap on top of her head approached the table.

'Greetings,' she said. 'I hear you want to speak to me.'

'Cerise?' asked Miranda, wiping her mouth on her napkin. The barmaid nodded.

'We're looking to find Tarakona Canyon.' Miranda took out a little drawstring bag of coins and placed it on the table, opening it so Cerise could see the gold inside.

Cerise nodded slowly. 'It's east of here.' She took a fountain pen from her breast pocket and sketched out a diagram on Miranda's napkin. 'The River Vaal runs through it. Mount Vaal and Mount Enoc are at either end. Look out for those and you won't go wrong. Careful though – they say Mount Vaal is still an active volcano.'

Miranda took the napkin and examined it. 'Most useful.'

Cerise leaned over the table to take Echo's empty plate. 'It's a popular place all of a sudden. You're the second band of sky pirates to ask about it today.'

'Oh really?' Miranda paused, her fork halfway from her mouth. 'And who was the first band?'

Cerise simpered. 'I don't think I can—'

BANG! Miranda stabbed the fork into the table, narrowly missing Cerise's fingers. She flipped back her cloak to show the barmaid the glittering pistol that was holstered on her hip. 'I think you'll find you can tell me anything I desire to know.'

Cerise froze, her face drained white with fear.

Behind her, the tavern door opened and Gilbert butted Echo's cheek with his nose.

Echo looked up and caught a glimpse of purple velvet and a glossy black plait. She stared for a moment and, as the woman's head turned so she could scan the room, she realized it was Rashmi the Ruthless, the leader of the Heartless Violet Pilots.

'Er, Miranda,' said Echo, tilting her head towards the tavern entrance.

Miranda took one glance at Rashmi and pocketed the map. 'Let's go.' She pulled the hood of her cloak low over her face and turned to Cerise, one hand still threateningly on her pistol. 'Is there a back door?'

Cerise nodded. 'This way.' She ducked her head and walked swiftly to the rear of the tavern, with Miranda and Echo close behind.

Miranda stormed through the boardwalk streets of Amaranth Point, Echo scurrying in her wake. 'Did she see us?' barked Miranda.

'I . . . I don't think so,' said Echo.

'Hurry then, we have no time to lose.' Miranda barged through the crowds of shoppers and waved her gun at the man at the gate.

Outside the town gates, a huge, ebony-wood sky galleon with three purple-silk balloons and a silver plaque inscribed PURPLE PEOPLE EATER was moored next to *Anaconda*.

'The cheek of it,' snarled Miranda. 'Let's see how Rashmi likes this.' She took her pistol and aimed it. *BANG!* She shot the first balloon. *BANG! BANG!* Each of the balloons in turn let out a hiss and began to sag. Miranda laughed. 'That should slow her down.'

'But . . . but that's not playing fair,' said Echo. 'Surely all the clans in the alliance should have a chance at the treasure?' She thought back to the bags of emeralds and gold in the cabinet of *Anaconda*. 'You have so much already.'

Miranda stared at Echo as though she was stupid. 'The Cutlass of Calinthe isn't just treasure,' she snapped. 'Whoever wields it is the leader of all the clans. Do you know what that means?'

'N . . . not really.'

'It means that I will unite all seven clans. All Seven Skies. Do you think I'm going to let that idiot Rashmi take charge? Or Old Gus? Or Indigo Lil? None of those fools can lead the seven skies like I can!'

Echo flushed with anger. 'But everyone should have their fair chance. You didn't have to puncture Rashmi's balloons.'

'I don't care about fair. I care about winning.' She glared at Echo, her green eyes flashing. 'And I don't need to hear about it from a little bit of dragon bait like you.'

Dragon bait? Echo's insides turned cold. So this was why Miranda had brought Echo with her. She wasn't going to help her at all.

'You're a liar and a cheat!'

Miranda shrugged and drew her cutlass with a *swish*. She pressed it to Echo's throat. 'I know, it's terribly unfair, isn't it? Now, back to your cabin where you can't cause any more trouble. I have a cutlass to find, and you are not going to stop me.'

She grabbed Echo by the collar of her shirt and marched her back inside *Anaconda* to her cabin, where she pushed her roughly inside. Echo heard the door slide across and the click of a lock, then the *Anaconda*'s engines roared and they were off, leaving the Mallow Marshes and the deflated balloons of the *Purple People Eater* far behind them.

CHAPTER TWENTY-TWO

When she was sure Miranda had gone, Echo tried the door, but it was firmly locked, no matter how hard she pushed and pulled. She slammed both fists against it in frustration. It had all been a huge mistake to trust Miranda. Old Gus had tricked her too. She should have known by now that the other clans weren't honest sky pirates like Lil and the Black Sky Wolves. They didn't care about fighting for good; they just cared about themselves!

Echo shook her head. She should have found another way back to the *Scarlet Margaret*. Her mother would have known what to do to get Horace back. A thought suddenly hit her like a thunderbolt. No wonder she hadn't had a message from Lil. Miranda hadn't sent the postal pigeon! She had lied about the whole thing! So now Echo was stuck here with a crazy woman and Lil had no idea where she was. She could feel a sob building in her chest, but she fought it back down and scrubbed her eyes furiously with her shirtsleeve. She wouldn't let Miranda make her cry.

She paced over to the bed and looked out of the porthole. They were leaving the pink haze of the Mallow Marshes behind now, but up ahead she could make out brownish mountains looming on the horizon. She leaned her head against the window, the glass cool against her brow, and clenched her fists. Some sky pirate she was. Lil would never have got herself into this mess! Why had Echo ever thought Miranda was going to help her?

They flew for hour after hour, and, the next time Echo peered out of the porthole, the brown mountains had become a vast reddish desert. Acres of rust-coloured dust spread out before her, studded here and there with wild, thorny trees and strange rock formations that arched into the air like giant ribcages. The land seemed to have rippled and folded in on itself, like a huge scarlet tablecloth that had been flung into the air, and, as they flew onwards, Echo saw the terrain was pocked with the craters of extinct volcanoes.

We're in the Dragonlands, she thought, with a shiver.

And then, when it was almost dusk and her belly was growling with hunger, she saw them – Mount Vaal and Mount Enoc – the two volcanoes marking the ends of the vast Tarakona Canyon, and the River Vaal weaving through its centre like a silver snake.

'Nearly there, Gilbert,' she said, turning to stroke the little lizard's chin. 'I wonder what we're going to find.'

There was a tap at the windowpane and Echo spun round in panic, half expecting to see Miranda's furious face looming over her. But what she saw made her heart soar with hope. It was her own postal pigeon, flying alongside the airship and trying in vain to get in through the porthole.

A message! It had to be from Lil. She must have found Echo's postal pigeon in her cabin on the *Scarlet Margaret* and known that it would be able to find her by homing in on her hairpin.

Echo gripped the porthole with both hands and rattled it, but it was no use. It didn't open at all. She cast round the room for something to break the glass, but there was nothing that could help her. Gilbert ran down her leg and nudged at her boot.

Of course! She grabbed *Stinger* from its scabbard and tried to prise the frame away, but the window was sturdy and ridiculously strong.

Echo flung the sword down in frustration 'Oh, how can I let it in?' she wailed.

Gilbert leaped on to the wall and peered out of the porthole, a perplexed expression on his scaly face.

Outside, the mechanical pigeon continued to keep pace with the airship, periodically diving towards the window, despite being tossed this way and that by the wind. But, however much Echo struggled with it, the window stayed firmly shut.

As the minutes passed, the little bird began to lose height. Echo watched in dismay as it was buffeted about, until finally it spiralled down towards the ground and disappeared from view.

'No!' Echo pressed her nose to the porthole, but no matter how hard she looked, the postal pigeon was gone.

She slammed her fist against the glass before flopping back on to her bunk, letting the tears of sadness and frustration roll down her cheeks. How long *could* a postal pigeon fly? And what would happen when its clockwork finally wound down? Would it just drop on to the ground, smashing into pieces, never to be found again? Echo squeezed her eyes shut and let the tears flow.

'Perhaps it will just return to sender,' she mumbled eventually.

Gilbert gave her an encouraging nudge on the shoulder with his snout.

'I know, Gilbert. We'll find a way to get Horace back somehow. I won't let anything bad happen to him.' Echo lay back on the bunk as Gilbert ran up to the porthole to peer out again. But even she had to admit that she had no idea how she was going to get out of the mess she'd made.

Gilbert gave a sudden chirrup, as if to say, *Look*.

'What is it?'

The little lizard had his front feet up on the rim of the porthole and was peering out intently.

Echo got to her feet, but there was a bang and the ship rocked, sending her crashing backwards on to the floor.

'Ouch!' she said, rubbing her elbow. 'What in all the seven skies is happening out there?'

She staggered to the porthole and gasped. A familiar shark-shaped airship hovered up ahead of them.

'*Obsidian!*' Echo exclaimed. They'd found it. And that meant they'd soon find Horace! She spun round, newly determined. 'Come on, Gilbert! We'll catch up with them soon. I do hope he's okay . . .'

There was another bang and the whole ship shuddered. 'Are

they *shooting* at us?' She dived back to the porthole, just in time to see a ball of orange flame shoot forward from beneath their ship. No, the *Thunder Sharks* weren't firing at *Anaconda*. *Miranda* was firing at *Obsidian*!

Echo staggered to one side as the ship dived downwards. Gilbert clung to the bedclothes and Echo's knapsack tumbled off the bunk, spilling its contents across the floor.

'Oh no! What is she doing?'

Fear froze Echo's heart as the ship lurched. If *Obsidian* crashed with Horace onboard . . . But she couldn't think about that now. She had to do something!

Echo raced to the door and rattled it again, but it was locked tight. She pressed the numbers on the keypad at random, but in vain. The pad just gave out an electronic bleep, and the door remained firmly closed.

She glanced across the floor at her scattered possessions and got down on her hands and knees to hurriedly pack them back into her knapsack. There had to be something among them that would help her. She threw in the jelly beans and the library card the librarian had given her. But, as she put her hand into the bag, she felt the silky threads of one of the aethernets run over her fingers.

The aethernet crackled with some remnant of thundercloud electricity and an idea hit Echo like a mini bolt of lightning. If she could just get the door-control panel open.

She went back to the door and examined the panel. 'What

do you think, Gilbert?' she said. 'Will it work?'

Gilbert bobbed his head encouragingly as Echo reached into her boot and drew out *Stinger*. For the first time, she was pleased not to have a full-sized cutlass. *Stinger* felt just right in her hand, light and slim, and the razor-sharp blade tip was slender enough to wedge into the joint where the cover of the control panel was attached. Echo pushed it in and levered the cover back a fraction. There was another rumble from below and the ship rocked as a volley of deafening cannon fire blasted out of *Anaconda* beneath her feet. Echo was ready for it this time though, and she braced herself against the door frame until the ship steadied.

Once it was still, she buried *Stinger* deep into the joint and levered the cover off with a *pop*. She re-sheathed *Stinger* and looked at the lock workings. They weren't like anything she'd ever seen before. She frowned. It seemed like a lifetime ago that she'd learned about clockwork with Jimmy Mainspring at the Mech Market in Port Tourbillon. But none of that old knowledge seemed to help. This wasn't clockwork – it was electronics. She gritted her teeth. Horace was in danger. She had to try.

She slung her knapsack over her shoulder, ready to make a quick getaway, then reached inside and closed her fingers round the shadowy filaments of the aethernet. She carefully drew it up and flung it at the wiring inside the control panel. There was a flurry of sparks and a bang. Gilbert's crest stood up on end and Echo sprang backwards, coughing as a cloud of foul-smelling smoke billowed from the panel.

As the smoke cleared, the ship rocked to the left and Echo pumped her fist in the air as the cabin door slowly slid open.

She stuffed the aethernet back into her knapsack and shoved *Stinger*'s scabbard into the side of her boot. She had to stop Miranda before something terrible happened to Horace.

CHAPTER TWENTY-THREE

Echo raced to the cockpit, Gilbert clinging to her shoulder. The whole airship rolled as Miranda fired the cannons again, and Echo fell to one side, slamming into the wall and almost dislodging Gilbert, who let out an indignant squeak.

Echo righted herself and stumbled to the cockpit doorway. Miranda had her back to Echo, and was leaning forward over the control deck, her long white fingers flying over the keys as she got her target in sight. There was a faint smell of gunpowder in the air and, through the viewscreen, Echo saw a smoking hole in the side of *Obsidian*.

'Stop!' Echo shouted.

Miranda turned in surprise. 'How did you . . . ?'

'Stop firing!' Echo's voice shook. She put her hands on her hips and tried to steady herself. 'Horace is onboard that ship.'

'I don't care who's onboard. They're not going to get that cutlass before me.'

Miranda turned her steely eyes to the viewscreen again and fired another volley of shots at *Obsidian*.

Echo raced forward and grabbed Miranda's sleeve.

'Get off me!' Miranda snatched her arm away. 'How dare you!'

'But you said you'd help me find him. You promised!'

Miranda ignored her. 'Did I? I forget.'

Echo took another panicked glance out of the viewscreen. *Obsidian* was tilting dangerously to one side and flying low above the river. There was a crackling of shots and Miranda yanked on the altimeter. Echo staggered back as *Anaconda* barrelled upwards and a cannonball whizzed past the windscreen.

'Ha!' Miranda wheeled *Anaconda* round. 'If Old Gus thinks he's going to find that cutlass first, he's mistaken. Let's see who's leader of the seven skies now, eh?'

Echo steadied herself on the dashboard. Miranda wouldn't listen to her. But she had to stop her somehow. If *Obsidian* went down with Horace on it . . . Echo couldn't bear to think about it. Her hand went to *Stinger* and she drew the blade from its scabbard with a *swish*. Warmth spread through her fingers and she felt a low thrum as *Stinger*'s hilt settled in her palm. 'Stop,' she said. 'Or I'll . . . I'll—'

'Ha!' Miranda turned to look at Echo. 'Or you'll what?'

Echo made a forward lunge, but Miranda was quicker. She drew her cutlass and blocked Echo's blade with one swift swipe of her own. The blow reverberated up Echo's arm, but she held tight to her sword and wrenched it away from Miranda's. Miranda advanced on Echo, a ferocious grin on her face, and swung her blade again.

Echo parried *Stinger* and their blades clanged together.

'A fighter, are you?' Miranda's cutlass flashed as she hacked at Echo.

'Yes, I am!' Echo quickly sidestepped, setting Miranda off-balance. The cutting edge of Miranda's blade bit into the *Anaconda*'s dashboard, sending sparks and chunks of metal flying across the cockpit.

Echo made a running attack, but Miranda's blade was longer and heavier and sharper. Miranda regained her balance and, with a final deft wrist-flick, sent *Stinger* spinning out of Echo's hand and across the floor.

Echo leaped across the cockpit towards her blade. She grabbed the little rapier and managed to scramble to her feet, but Miranda was on top of her with the razor-sharp edge of her cutlass to Echo's throat.

'Nice try,' said Miranda, with a grimace. 'Seems I do need to relieve you of your sword after all.'

'No!' The blade was sharp against Echo's throat. She leaned backwards, but she was right up against the control deck. She reached a hand behind her, inadvertently grabbing a lever to steady herself. *Anaconda* seemed to suddenly drop out of the sky.

Miranda let out a yelp and fell backwards as the ship nosedived towards the water. She shoved Echo out of the way and grappled with the controls as they dropped out of the sky. Below them, Echo saw *Obsidian* stranded on the side of the canyon, its balloon rapidly deflating and its crew spilling from emergency exits and scattering among the smoke and flames.

Horace! Echo's chest clenched. She scanned the wreckage, but she couldn't see him through the rubble and smoke. She had to find him. What if he was hurt?

She stumbled as Miranda righted the ship and they flew out low across the open water of the river. Echo's eyes alighted on the triangular golden button on the dashboard. Could she do it? There was only one way to find out. She made a run for it. *BANG!* She hammered the button with her fist.

Miranda turned, her mouth open. 'What are you doing . . . ?'

But Echo was already across the cockpit and at the trapdoor as it slid open.

'Come back here! You can't—'

'Watch me!' Echo stuffed *Stinger* into her boot, held her knapsack tight with one hand and Gilbert with the other.

And she jumped.

CHAPTER TWENTY-FOUR

Echo clutched Gilbert to her chest as she tumbled out of *Anaconda* and plummeted through the air. The river below rushed towards her and for a terrible moment she thought, *What if it's not deep enough? What if my brains are dashed out on rocks, or I break all my bones, or I—*

The rushing air took her breath away and the fall was over all too quickly as she plunged into ice-cold water. The outside world was suddenly muffled as she sank into the blue-grey depths. She stretched her arms out and kicked her legs, fighting against the weight of her wet clothes and the knapsack and Gilbert, who was still clinging tightly to her shoulder. Echo's lungs burned. She kicked harder and struggled to the surface, bursting out of the water with a gasp and gulping greedy lungfuls of air. Gilbert shook himself and snorted spray from his nose.

Echo coughed up a mouthful of water and bobbed, panting, on the surface. Above her, *Anaconda* was whirring away, still firing at *Obsidian*, which lay beached on the slope of the canyon, keeling drunkenly to one side.

Echo got her breath back and positioned Gilbert on her head. She set out for the riverbank, and *Obsidian*, and Horace.

There was a *whoosh* and something white shot past Echo, hitting the water with a fizzling splash. She glanced up at *Anaconda* and realized with horror that a stray cannonball had almost hit her. *Obsidian* fired its own blast from where it lay wrecked. Further out, on the horizon, Echo could see yet another airship arriving. Some other sky-pirate clans must have got wind of the location of the treasure. Among the chaos, a flare of hope lit in Echo's heart. Did that mean Lil and the others would be on their way too?

But there wasn't time to think, as another rapid burst of fire erupted from *Anaconda's* cannons. Echo had to get to safety! She'd never save Horace or find Lil if she got herself killed.

'Hold your breath!' she shouted to Gilbert, before diving into the water.

More missiles plunged into the river centimetres away from them and Echo almost gulped in a mouthful of water as the cannonballs shot past. She held her breath and swam onwards. Up ahead was a partially submerged rock, and she kicked out for it with all her strength, her lungs and limbs burning. When she could hold her breath no longer, she finally dared to pop her head up, and lifted Gilbert out too. They both floated, gasping for breath, close to the rust-coloured rock.

Above them, *Anaconda* circled the helpless wreck of *Obsidian*, which lay motionless on one side and was emitting plumes of black smoke.

'Come on,' whispered Echo.

She quietly withdrew to the far side of the rock, so she was shielded from view. Gilbert paddled ahead of her, before scrambling on to the rock and shaking water from his scales. Echo didn't dare emerge just yet, but clung to the lichen-clad surface with her fingertips, watching and waiting until *Obsidian*'s cannons finally juddered to a halt and *Anaconda* buzzed away.

Once *Anaconda* was out of sight, Echo swam to the riverbank and dragged herself out, sopping wet. She lay panting for several minutes, rivulets of water running from her clothes and hair. When she'd recovered, she raised her head and squinted up at the wreck of *Obsidian*, which lay further up the canyon wall. The Thunder Sharks swarmed all over it, flinging buckets of water and sand at the many fires. But where was Horace? Echo took out her spyglass and scanned the canyon side. She couldn't see him anywhere, but she could make out a dense clump of thorn bushes below the line of sight of the Thunder Sharks. It looked like a good place to hide where she wouldn't be spotted.

As Echo crept closer up the side of the canyon, she saw that *Obsidian* was almost destroyed. Its metallic sides were dented and blackened, its balloon wilted sadly and its tail fin had snapped off and lay in pieces in the dust.

The blue-clad Thunder Sharks ran here and there, starting to make repairs to the stricken ship. Echo spotted Stanley wielding a bucket of tar and Mei doling hammers out to the other crew members. But Echo could see that they wouldn't be patching *Obsidian* up in a hurry.

Gilbert gave a sudden squeak of recognition and, as Echo watched, she saw a familiar blond mop of hair among the many others.

'Horace,' she whispered. 'Oh, thank the seven skies he's okay.'

She crept forward through the thorny bushes as far as she dared.

Horace seemed to be collecting pieces of debris from where they were strewn across the ground. Echo willed him to come close enough to hear her, but, just as he started walking towards her, he spotted something on the ground and knelt to examine it.

'Horace,' Echo hissed. But he didn't hear her. He picked up whatever it was, turned and walked away again.

Echo sighed in exasperation. How could she get his attention? She rooted in her bag and found the parchment with the riddle on it that Old Gus had given her and the remains of the paper bag of jelly beans.

Gilbert opened his mouth expectantly.

'Okay, but just one,' said Echo. 'I'll need the rest.'

Gilbert gulped down a purple jelly bean and his tail curled up in delight.

Echo rolled the parchment into a tube, then shuffled forward as far as she dared, careful to keep hidden.

Horace came back over, his eyes on the ground. When he got closer, Echo raised the paper tube to her lips, inserted a pink jelly bean in the end and blew.

The jelly bean flew through the air and landed on the stones a metre away from Horace's boots.

Gilbert took one look at the pink sweet and raced after it.

'Gilbert, no!' Echo's heart seemed to jump into her throat as the little lizard ran across the rocks, his golden scales gleaming against the reddish ground.

'Gilbert!' Horace jerked his head up in surprise. 'What are you doing here?'

He glanced around and scooped Gilbert up in his hands. Gilbert jabbed his tail in Echo's direction.

Horace took a quick look over his shoulder, then darted over to where Echo was hiding. He flung himself down next to her.

'Echo!' he said. He threw his arms round her in a hug, then hurriedly backed away. 'You're drenched!'

'Are you okay?' Echo felt so relieved to finally find him she was almost dizzy. She moved back for a moment to look him over. 'You're not hurt, are you?'

'Me? No, just a few bumps and bruises when that other ship attacked us. What happened to you? How did you find me?'

'It's kind of a long story,' said Echo, with a smile. 'How about you?'

Horace grimaced. 'I can't say being a Thunder Shark agrees with me, but I'm still in one piece. They've mostly had me learning facts about dragons from a load of ancient books. Old Gus isn't a big reader.' He looked at her. 'So what's the plan?'

'I didn't have time to make a plan,' said Echo, explaining her hurried free-fall exit from *Anaconda*.

'Horace! Where is that boy?' There was an exasperated shout from one of the Thunder Sharks and Horace paled.

'They're looking for me,' he said.

'Let's go,' said Echo.

'But where?'

Echo shrugged. 'Not sure, but I guess the first thing we should do is get away from here. Come on.'

She scrambled off back down the canyon, with Horace skidding along close behind her.

CHAPTER TWENTY-FIVE

Soon the Thunder Sharks' voices faded as Echo and Horace clambered further down the canyon side. The sun was setting below the high canyon wall and the evening chill made Echo shiver. At least *Obsidian* was out of action and *Anaconda* had disappeared for the moment.

'We need to find somewhere to hide while we figure out what to do,' said Echo, as they made their way back down to the riverbank, where a series of rocks formed stepping stones to the other side. 'There must be a cave or something we can spend the night in.'

She took out her spyglass and scanned the soaring cliffs, with their stripey layers of reddish rock. A few hundred metres away, a waterfall tumbled its way down the side of the ravine and, partway down, Echo saw the darkness of a hidden cave.

'There!' she said, pointing and handing the spyglass to Horace.

Soon they were hidden safely inside the cave, its only inhabitants being a colony of large, furry bats, who eyed them sleepily from their upside-down perches on the ceiling. Echo gathered some dry sticks from the bushes outside and Horace made a small fire in an alcove where it wouldn't be spotted by the Thunder Sharks from across the canyon. Opening her knapsack, Echo found the marshmallows she'd picked outside Amaranth Point and passed a handful to Horace.

'Thanks,' he said, spiking one with a stick and holding it over the flames. 'I haven't had anything except boiled gulls' eggs and sky biscuits for weeks.'

'Sky biscuits?' Echo frowned, remembering seeing them once at the Mech Market in Port Tourbillon. 'Do they taste nice?'

'Not at all,' said Horace, with a grimace. 'They're full of weevils.'

Echo pulled a face of her own and bit into a hot, molten marshmallow.

'What happened to you?' asked Horace. 'I know you found the map.'

Echo explained her adventures as they munched on the rest of the sticky treats. 'Miranda's dying to get her hands on the

Cutlass of Calinthe,' she said. 'It's not as if she needs any more treasure. She's just desperate to be the leader of the seven skies.'

'They all want it,' said Horace. 'Old Gus too. He said all the other clans would have to bow down to him and follow his orders. He gets a horrible look in his eye when he talks about it.'

Bow down to him? Echo swallowed. Miranda had said something about uniting the seven skies. But she hadn't been talking about bringing them together – she wanted to rule over all of them! Echo shuddered. Would the Black Sky Wolves have to bow down to her too? And what terrible things would Miranda do with all seven pirate clans in her command and nobody to stop her?

'Echo, what is it? You've gone awfully pale.' Horace looked around nervously. 'It's not a dragon, is it?'

'No, no dragons.' She shook herself. They couldn't sit here worrying. She had to do something, but what? Lil would know.

'We need to get a message to Lil and the rest of the Black Sky Wolves,' Echo said.

If only I'd been able to see where Miranda kept her postal pigeons, she thought in dismay. But then an idea occurred to her. 'Were there any postal parrots aboard *Obsidian*?'

Horace puffed out his cheeks. 'There was a store of them in the navigation room—'

'Perfect!'

Horace shook his head. 'You didn't let me finish. They all

got destroyed by one of Miranda's missiles.'

'All of them?'

Horace nodded glumly. 'I saw it myself. Blown to bits. They're quite flammable, you know, with that self-destruct function.'

Echo sighed. She was all out of ideas. 'Oh, what are we going to do?' she said. 'We have to stop them somehow.'

'We can't, Echo. We're just kids and they're sky pirates.'

'I'm a sky pirate too.' Echo scowled.

There was the faint buzz of an airship engine and Horace jerked his head up anxiously.

In the distance, Echo saw *Anaconda* pull in and land at the far end of the canyon, near the smoke-scorched crater of Mount Enoc. Echo shrank back, praying Miranda hadn't seen them sneak into the cave.

A metallic, fluttering sound made her jump and suddenly her postal pigeon burst through the waterfall.

Echo gasped and jumped up to catch the little mechanical bird in both hands. 'You weren't lost after all!' She turned to Horace. 'It must be a message from my mother!'

'Brilliant!' Horace's face filled with relief.

Echo unrolled the little tube of parchment clasped in the bird's claw, trying to stop her hands from shaking. She held it up to the firelight and read the message.

Echo, where are you and Horace? Frantic with worry.

Please respond. Lil

Echo's heart clenched with relief.

'What're you going to say?' asked Horace after she'd shown him the note.

She blinked back tears and cleared her throat. They were lost in the Dragonlands, on the run, and trapped between rival pirate clans all desperate for the Cutlass of Calinthe. How *could* she say everything she wanted to on such a small scrap of paper? In the end, she scrawled a brief message to Lil.

Stranded at Tarakona Canyon in the Dragonlands. Beware - Thunder Sharks and Scurvy Sea Snakes here, maybe others too. Echo. PS Sorry!

She would just have to explain everything properly when Lil and the others arrived.

Echo rolled up the paper and tucked the message into the postal pigeon's claw, then wound its clockwork and turned the dials to set it to fly to the *Scarlet Margaret's* navigation point. She threw the little bird up into the air and it whirred away. She kept watching until it disappeared into the darkness.

Horace looked at her. 'How long do you think it'll take them to get here?'

Echo shrugged. 'I don't know. I guess it depends where they

are now. It took us a couple of days from the Aqualiber Vaults.'

'You're right. I suppose we just wait here until then.' Horace sat down beside her.

'Do you think Miranda will find the cutlass?' asked Echo. 'She doesn't know the way into the dragon cave.'

'Neither do the Thunder Sharks,' said Horace. 'But we saw claw marks and scorching round the rim of Mount Enoc when we were flying over. I think the dragon lives inside the cone. There must be all kinds of caverns and lava tubes inside.'

Echo nodded. 'I wonder if there's another way in.'

'What do you mean?'

'Well, it's kind of obvious going in the dragon's front door.'

'You wouldn't catch me going in *any* door belonging to a dragon.' Horace shivered. 'Have you got anything else to eat?' he asked. 'These marshmallows are nice, but I'm starving.'

Echo emptied out her knapsack on to the rocks. 'Just these jelly beans,' she said. 'But I think we should ration them in case we get desperate.' She picked up the compass. 'I found this old compass with the map in the Aqualiber Vaults,' she said. 'It doesn't seem to work though. It points somewhere, but it doesn't seem to be north.'

'Maybe you can fix it when we get back to the *Scarlet Margaret*,' said Horace. 'You're good at that sort of stuff.'

Echo shrugged and frowned at the silver compass. What was wrong with it? She took the pin from her hair and carefully prised the back loose. She eased the casing open and, to her surprise, saw that the insides were exactly like the mechanism of her postal pigeon. It was a navigation device!

'Horace, look!' She waved the compass at him.

'What is it?' Horace peered at the mechanism by the light of the fire. 'It's very . . . er, nice and shiny?'

'No, that's not what I'm showing you. This isn't an ordinary compass!'

Horace frowned. 'So what is it?'

Echo hugged herself, barely able to stop the excitement from fizzing out of her. 'It's a clue! It doesn't point north. It points to the dragon's cave!' Echo said, a huge grin spreading across her face. 'It was wrapped up in the map that Old Gus has, but none of them know about this part!'

'So that means . . .'

'It means that Old Gus and Miranda won't be able to find the way into the dragon's lair.'

'Phew!' Horace slumped down with a sigh. 'So we don't have to stop them then. That's a relief!'

'Yes,' said Echo. 'I think the Cutlass of Calinthe is safe. Unless they do manage to get through the dragon's front door, that is.'

'I don't think that's likely,' said Horace, with a snort. 'A mountain dragon's breath is as powerful as a volcano!'

Echo nodded.

'So we'll just hide out here until the *Scarlet Margaret* arrives,' said Horace.

'Yes,' said Echo. But thoughts of treasure and adventures had made something else start to bubble up inside her. Neither Old Gus nor Miranda knew where to find the entrance to the dragon's lair, but she and Horace did. And ... did she even dare think it? Maybe they would be able to get the Cutlass of Calinthe before the others. That way they would know it was safe from Miranda and Old Gus. And, when Lil got there, Echo could prove herself as a real sky pirate at last!

She glanced at the compass again. Its needles jittered. Echo frowned. 'Look.' She pointed to the face. The needles wobbled and spun again. 'Why would they do that?' she said.

'It's obviously broken,' said Horace, yawning. 'Maybe it got magnetized accidentally somehow.'

'No.' Echo frowned. 'This is no accident.'

'Whatever you say,' said Horace, settling down to sleep by the fire.

Echo stood up and walked in the direction the needles were pointing. As she walked, they jittered and wobbled beneath the glass.

She turned the little compass over and over, peering into its clockwork. A shard of jelly bean was jammed between one of the navigation wheels and the ratchet. She used her little finger to work it loose. There was a whirring noise and the compass sprang open like a music box, but, instead of a ballerina, a tiny golden dragon popped up, a miniature cutlass between its teeth.

'Look!' breathed Echo.

There was no answer.

Echo glanced up to find Horace had fallen asleep and was breathing softly.

She turned back to the gleaming golden dragon, its scales shimmering in the light of the fire.

'A dragon holding the Cutlass of Calinthe!' she whispered in wonder. 'And I think it's showing us the way.'

CHAPTER TWENTY-SIX

The next morning, Echo woke to find that the fire had burned down to glowing coals and the early-morning sun was slanting through the waterfall, casting little rainbows on the cave walls. Horace was still fast asleep and snoring softly. Gilbert had taken inspiration from the bats and was hanging upside down from the cave roof as he stalked a juicy-looking fly.

Echo wandered to the mouth of the cave and looked out beyond the rushing water and across the canyon. On the other side, the Thunder Sharks were still working diligently on *Obsidian*. Overnight, its tail had been reattached and she could see a group of pirates patching up the deflated balloon envelope. Soon they'd be on their way to the dragon's lair . . . and the cutlass.

Echo suddenly remembered last night's discovery and pulled the compass from her pocket. She flicked open the case and held it out in front of her. As she did so, the tiny golden dragon spun round so its nose was pointing southwards down the canyon, towards Mount Enoc. The way to the Cutlass of Calinthe.

Echo stole a guilty glance at Horace. She knew in her heart that he would never agree to them going after the cutlass by themselves. But they simply had to. If it got into Miranda's hands, or Old Gus's, or any of them, the Black Sky Wolves would be under their command. Echo shuddered. With someone like Miranda in charge of seven sky-pirate clans, the whole world would be in danger. No, there was nothing for it. She had to try and get it herself, and, if that meant telling a white lie to her best friend in the world, that was what she must do. She scanned the canyon again. At least there were only two clans of sky pirates they needed to avoid, and the Thunder Sharks weren't on the move quite yet.

'Morning,' said Horace, appearing beside her and stretching.

'Morning.' Echo shoved the compass back in her pocket.

They splashed their faces with icy water from the waterfall and drank from cupped hands. As the water hit Echo's stomach, it growled with hunger. 'We really need to find some food,' she said.

Horace took the spyglass and scanned the canyon. After a few moments, he grinned. 'Look,' he said, pointing and passing the spyglass to Echo. 'I'm sure pitaya are edible. The professor had some pickled ones in his pantry!'

'Pitaya?' asked Echo.

'Also known as dragon fruit.'

Echo took a look through the spyglass and saw bright pink fruits growing on a cactus down on the canyon floor. Her mouth watered. This could be the perfect breakfast.

And the perfect reason to get Horace out of hiding and closer to Mount Enoc, Echo thought guiltily. 'Let's go!' she said.

After scrambling over boulders and down slopes of loose rust-coloured shale, Echo and Horace soon found the dragon-fruit cactus and collected a haul of the juicy pink-skinned fruit.

Echo perched next to Horace on a boulder, warmed by the morning sun, and peeled off the prickly skin of a dragon fruit. She bit into the juicy white flesh. The fruit was sweet and studded with tiny black seeds that crunched between her teeth. They both ate greedily and looked out across the canyon. The air was calm, with just the rush of the river and the wind whistling over the reddish stone walls to break the silence. Occasionally, a bird of prey would circle high above them, its cry ringing out across the stillness of the valley below. Echo licked her sticky fingers and watched Gilbert as he stalked an unsuspecting grasshopper. Suddenly he looked up and froze, his scales turning danger red.

'What is it?' Echo looked up too. She couldn't see anything, but, as she stood perfectly still, she could just make out the faint buzz of airship engines in the distance. Her heart soared. Could it be the *Scarlet Margaret*?

'There,' said Horace, pointing, his forehead creased with worry. At the far end of the canyon, the dark shape of an airship was getting larger. But it wasn't the *Scarlet Margaret*, Echo saw, as the ship sailed closer. As it flew overhead, bathing them in shadow, she took in its billowing ochre sails emblazoned with a black scorpion. Echo thought back to the meeting of the Seven Skies Alliance, and Steel-eyed Seth in his yellow jerkin. It had to be the Stormshakers' ship!

Yet another band of sky pirates on the hunt for the Cutlass of Calinthe, she realized in despair.

Once the ship was gone, Echo took out the compass and held it in front of her. The little dragon was still pointing south to the extinct volcano.

'You don't still think that thing's a clue, do you?'

Echo shrugged. 'I don't know. But what I do know is we should head for Mount Enoc.'

'But that's where all the other pirates are,' said Horace, his mouth falling open in horror. 'That's the last place I'd want to go!'

'But that's where Lil will go,' said Echo, quickly thinking up a reason that Horace might like. She gestured at the volcano cone, where *Anaconda* was moored and the yellow-sailed ship was fast approaching. 'It's the most obvious place to wait.'

'It's the most dangerous place to wait,' said Horace.

'We'll keep hidden,' said Echo. 'Trust me.'

'I always do, Echo. And we always get into trouble.'

'But we always get out again too.' Echo softened her voice. 'Please, Horace. I know how Lil thinks,' she said. 'The closer we get, the better. Anyway, the other pirates will all be going inside the volcano.' She braced herself for the lie. 'We'll stay outside, where we're safe.'

Horace thought for a moment. 'I suppose you're right,' he said.

Echo smiled in relief. 'Let's stick to the riverbank – there are more rocks to hide behind there.'

She pocketed the compass and strode off towards the sound of the river, before Horace could see the guilt that was etched all over her face.

They followed the riverbank as it wove across the canyon floor, pushing through patches of thorny shrubs that pulled on their clothes, climbing over reddish-brown boulders and tripping on animal bones. By the time they reached the foot of Mount Enoc, the sun was beating down on them from high overhead, and two more airships were circling close to the volcano's slopes.

Echo squinted up at them. The first was a neat copper ship with a lozenge-shaped orange balloon, and the second was a dark-wood galleon with blood-red sails and a huge chimney that belched out black smoke. *That only left the* Scarlet Margaret *and the* Purple People Eater *to arrive*, Echo thought. *Then all seven clans would be here to fight it out for the cutlass.*

'Well, this is it,' said Horace, gazing up at the slope of Mount Enoc with a shudder. He glanced around. 'We'd better find somewhere to hide until we spot the *Scarlet Margaret*.'

He ducked down in the shade of an overhanging ledge, out of sight of the gathering airships. Nearby, the river had widened into a circular pool, which swirled as the current entered it, and narrowed to a thin ribbon again before curving away round the base of the volcano. Echo settled down next to him and took out the compass.

'That's strange.' Echo frowned at the golden dragon. Before it had been clearly pointing at Mount Enoc, but now it was spinning in lazy circles, never settling on one direction.

'What is?' said Horace, his eyes closed.

'Look.' Echo showed him the compass. 'It's spinning.'

'Compasses do that when they get close to magnetic north,' said Horace.

A thought occurred to Echo. If a compass spun round when it got close to magnetic north, then this device might spin when it got close to where it wanted them to go. She took a few experimental steps. As she got closer to the pool, the little dragon spun faster.

She stood on the bank, searching for any kind of opening. As she watched, she saw that the water seemed to be draining into a large hole at the far end, like bathwater flowing down a plughole. Echo scrambled across the rocks to take a closer look. The hole was dark and steep, with several centimetres of water flowing down it. She checked the compass. The miniature dragon jittered and flicked back and forth, faster and faster, like it was alive. As she got even closer to the opening, the tiny figure did a nosedive so that it was pointing straight down.

Echo shook her head. 'No doubt about it, the only way is down,' she murmured.

'What are you doing over there?' Echo looked up to see Horace gingerly picking his way over the rocks to her. They both looked down into the hole, then at each other.

'It's a lava tube,' said Horace. 'It must have been formed when Mount Enoc was still active. I expect the whole mountain's riddled with them.'

'It's the way in,' said Echo, showing him the pocket watch.

'The way in to wher— Oh no!' said Horace, paling. 'A dragon's cave, Echo? Why would you even *want* to ...' He shook his head, aghast and lost for words.

Echo looked at Horace and thought for a moment. 'Don't you want to see a real dragon?' she said. 'Imagine what the professor would say! You'd be able to present your findings to the Explorers' Guild.'

'Never.' Horace folded his arms tightly across his chest. 'It's a bad idea, Echo. Very bad. I don't even like the look of that hole, and that's probably the best of it.'

'It'll be fine,' said Echo, keeping her voice light. 'It's just like the slideway at the professor's house.'

'But where does it end? In a dragon's lair? In a dragon's jaws? We'd get burned to a crisp or eaten, or burned *and* eaten.' He shook his head firmly. 'Absolutely not.'

'There's no time to argue,' hissed Echo. 'We need to get down there before the others find the cutlass. There are bigger things at stake.'

'I'm not arguing.' Horace folded his arms tightly across his chest. 'I'm refusing to get drawn into yet another one of your schemes. Dragons aren't to be trifled with, Echo. I've been reading all about them, remember? They're frightfully dangerous.'

'We'll be fine,' said Echo. She had to stop the other sky pirates before it was too late. And she couldn't let being frightened hold her back. 'Come on,' she said. She glanced up at the airships circling. 'If we stay out here, we're bound to get caught by the other sky pirates. We'll go together.'

Horace shook his head. 'No. I'm sorry, Echo. I'm hiding here until the Black Sky Wolves arrive—'

BANG! A deafening blast came from overhead as *Obsidian* came diving towards them, fire flaring from its cannons. Echo instinctively ducked as a stray cannonball plunged on to the rocks on the other side of the pool, smashing the ledge they'd been hiding under to smithereens. One of the other ships returned fire.

Horace put both hands over his head and crouched, shaking, on the riverbank.

Echo looked from him to *Obsidian*, wheeling above them, to the lava tube.

Without another word, she grabbed Horace's hand and jumped.

CHAPTER TWENTY-SEVEN

Echo landed with a bump and skidded down the tube on her bottom, pulling Horace behind her. A slimy carpet of weed cushioned their landing and the shallow trickle of water that flowed down the base of the tunnel swooshed them along into the darkness. With each twist and turn of the tunnel, they skidded up the sides and back down again, until Echo was quite dizzy.

'That was close!' she yelled, above the *whoosh* of the water.

'You tricked me!' Horace's voice wobbled with fear. 'You shouldn't have done that. We'll be eaten alive.'

'Safer down here than up there.'

'We'll see about that,' Horace whimpered.

Still the tunnel went on, going down and down into the heart of Mount Enoc. Soon it was pitch-black and still they kept sliding.

'If only we had the glow jar,' Echo shouted back over her shoulder. 'Then we could see where we're going.'

'I don't think I want to see,' said Horace. 'Oh, who knows what's down here?'

'Wait, I *can* see something.' Echo blinked. There was a dim blueish light in the tunnel up ahead. She could see the next bend. As they got closer, she saw the ceiling was covered in some kind of glowing blue mould. 'Look at this!' she yelled, as they whizzed past.

'What?' said Horace.

'On the ceiling!' Echo turned to look at back at him and saw his eyes were squeezed shut. 'Look up, Horace!'

He dared to open one eye and squinted up at the ceiling, then gasped. 'How fascinating,' he said. 'Phosphorescent lichen.'

Echo pushed herself upwards and leaped for the ceiling, grabbing at the lichen with both hands. She managed to rip a handful free before coming crashing down and spinning on the slippery tunnel floor.

'Try to get some, Horace!' she shouted, as she slid down the tunnel, now head first and on her back, clutching the fluffy, glowing fronds to her chest.

Horace reached for the lichen himself and managed to snatch a bunch with both hands. As Echo rocketed round another bend, she saw him dangle for a moment, before the lichen tore off and he tumbled back down into the tunnel and careered helter-skelter after her.

'When will this tunnel end?' he panted.

Echo swung her legs round and righted herself as she

kept sliding. Her heart was racing from a strange mixture of excitement and fear. They'd escaped the other sky pirates, but what was waiting for them at the bottom of the tunnel? And how would they ever find their way out again?

As they rounded yet another bend, Echo suddenly realized that their crazy descent was slowing. She could sit upright now, and the walls still flew past, but she wasn't being flung around every time they turned a corner or shot up the side of the tunnel when it spiralled in on itself.

'I think it's levelling off!' she shouted back to Horace.

They slid round one final bend and, in the light of the glowing lichen, Echo saw the tunnel opened into a wide greenish pool of water. Her heart fluttered with relief at the lack of dragons or anything else waiting to eat them. She whooshed down the final straight.

'Hold tight!' she shouted. 'I think we're going to—'

The pool swallowed Echo as she hit it with a splash. She bobbed up again and blinked. Horace popped up next to her, coughing up water. Gilbert swam a leisurely lizard-paddle in circles round them.

'Now what?' said Horace, glancing around nervously. He shivered. 'It's spooky down here.'

Echo took in their surroundings. The pool was in the centre of a wide, high-roofed cavern. The ceiling here was covered in the same glowing lichen that they'd found in the tunnel and the light cast eerie shadows on the water. Echo could make out another tunnel opening on the far wall, and two more to their left.

'I guess we take one of these,' she said.

'But which one?'

They waded out of the pool and on to the rocky cavern floor. Gilbert sneezed water from his nostrils and Horace wrung out his sopping shirtsleeves. Echo glanced around. Stalactites hung from the ceiling and water ran from their points with a steady *drip drip drip*. The cavern was cool and smelled of wet stone and pondweed.

Echo reached into her bag. 'Maybe the compass will help,' she said. She clicked open its silver casing and examined the face. The dragon wobbled and spun for a moment before settling.

'It's pointing here.' Echo traced the line. The compass seemed to be directing them to the two left-hand tunnels, but which one? 'Come on,' she said.

Gilbert clambered up her leg to find his perch on her shoulder and they crept forward into the furthest tunnel, bunches of glowing lichen held aloft.

They hadn't been walking long when there was a whooping, hooting sound from up ahead. Horace jumped and dropped his lichen bunch in shock.

Echo froze. 'What was that?' In her haste to get down here and find the dragon's lair, she hadn't considered there might be other creatures around too.

Gilbert's claws tightened on Echo's shoulder and he let out a tiny chirrup that Echo knew meant, *Oh no, owls!*

'You're right. I think it is owls,' she said.

'Are ... are you sure it's not ghosts?' said Horace, worry etched on his face.

Echo rolled her eyes. 'Don't be ridiculous. There's no such thing as ghosts.'

Horace flushed. 'It sounded spooky. I don't like it.'

'*Shh!*' Echo raised a finger to quieten him. It wasn't owls at all, but voices. A tingle of fear ran down her spine. The other sky pirates! They didn't have much time.

'Echo, we should get out of here.'

'Well, what do you suggest?' Echo hissed. 'We can't go back up the lava tube – it's too steep. Even if we could get all the way back up, we'd be caught by the other pirates outside and then where would we be?'

'We could go back and try a different tunnel.'

'But the dragon is pointing this way.'

Horace huffed. 'How do you know that thing's even working?'

'I just know, okay? Look, we're going to figure out a way to get the cutlass. Once we have that, the other sky pirates will have to do our bidding. But we don't have much time.'

Horace wrung his hands. 'We can't face a dragon. They're dangerous, and clever too. Nobody ever managed to take gold from under a dragon's nose. Not even the Knights of Nordland.'

Echo thought for a moment. 'There must be something you've learned from all your reading. Don't dragons ever leave their lairs to hunt?'

Horace thought for a moment. 'Yes, but not until night-time. They're nocturnal.'

'Couldn't we sneak in now while it's asleep?'

'No!'

'Well, there must be a way,' said Echo, although privately she had to admit that the whole thing seemed impossibly dangerous. But something inside her wouldn't let her give up and she kept on walking, into the eerie quiet of the tunnels. The pirate voices seemed to have faded away, and the only sound was the squelch of their soggy boots on stone and the thud of Echo's heart in her ears.

CHAPTER TWENTY-EIGHT

Echo and Horace trudged through the tunnels for what seemed like hours, following the direction of the compass dragon.

'Can we take a break?' Horace begged. 'We've been walking for ages.'

Echo looked round at him and took in the dark shadows under his eyes. 'I suppose so,' she said grudgingly. 'But just a short one. We need to keep moving.'

They hadn't heard any more shouts from the other sky pirates, but Echo couldn't help feeling nervous about their proximity. And what if Miranda or one of the others got to the Cutlass of Calinthe first? Echo couldn't let that happen.

They found a smooth area of the tunnel and sat down side by side in the gloom. Echo opened her knapsack and pulled out the bag of jelly beans, which they shared in companionable silence.

When they were finished, Echo tossed the last jelly bean

to Gilbert, who swallowed it with a gulp. She crumpled up the paper bag, shoved it back in her knapsack and got to her feet. 'We need to find this dragon cave before the others do. Come on.'

'Why do you really want to find it?' Horace said.

'To stop Miranda getting her hands on the cutlass, of course,' said Echo.

Horace shook his head. 'I mean the real reason. You can't be prepared to take something from under a dragon's nose just to stop Miranda getting her way. It's stealing.'

Echo felt her cheeks grow hot with indignation. 'That dragon has a whole hoard of treasure. It won't miss one measly cutlass.'

Horace frowned. 'I can't believe you'd risk getting burned to a crisp just to get some gold. What are you trying to prove?'

That I'm a real sky pirate, thought Echo. She folded her arms. 'I'm a Black Sky Wolf. Steal for good, that's our motto.'

'But you're not stealing for good.' Horace stared at her. 'You're just trying to impress your mother.'

'No, I'm not.' Echo glared at Horace, furious at both him and herself.

But Horace hadn't finished. 'If you steal from the dragon, you're just as bad as Vossberg and Old Gus and all the others,' he said.

'How?' exclaimed Echo. 'I'm not hurting anyone.'

'What about the dragon?'

'They're vicious monsters.'

'Says who? According to my studies, they're much misunderstood creatures that need our protection,' Horace exclaimed. 'Not that Old Gus listened to any of that,' he added ruefully.

'And who wrote that?'

'I don't know.' Horace sighed. 'Who told *you* they were vicious?'

It was Echo's turn to be embarrassed. 'Miranda,' she said.

'Exactly,' said Horace, with a huff. 'You might be desperate to be a sky pirate, but don't start acting like her.'

'I'm not desperate!' Echo folded her arms. But somewhere deep down she had to admit that Horace might be right.

After walking in grumpy silence for a while, Echo suddenly thought of something. 'Did your books say anything about communicating with dragons?' she asked. 'Maybe, if we talk to it, we can explain about the cutlass.'

Horace shook his head. 'They're known to be intelligent, but nobody's ever managed to talk to one and live to tell the tale,' he said. 'I'm sorry, Echo. I just don't think it'll work—'

But Horace didn't get a chance to finish his sentence. As they rounded the next bend, they both sucked in an awestruck breath. The tunnel had opened out into a vast cavern filled with gold from wall to wall. Mounds of gleaming coins, jewel-encrusted crowns, sceptres and swords lay heaped. Ropes of pearls were strewn among chests spilling over with gold doubloons.

And among all these riches, red-scales gleaming, tail curled round itself and smoke curling delicately from its nostrils, lay an enormous, sleeping dragon. A real dragon! Echo's head spun for a moment, not quite believing it, as she took in the sheer wonder of the huge red beast. As much as she'd been expecting it, preparing for it, dreading it almost, a small part of her hadn't quite believed that the dragon would be real. But here it was, breathing softly. It was breathtakingly enormous too, almost half the length of the *Scarlet Margaret*. Echo couldn't stop staring in awe. She could almost feel the power rising off the dragon in waves. It was beautiful. Dangerous but beautiful.

As they watched, the great creature stretched in its sleep, snorted out a tiny ring of smoke and refolded its wings. Horace covered his mouth with both hands to stifle a scream. Echo merely froze. For, when the dragon had shifted, it had lifted up its cream-scaled belly, revealing a clutch of three glittering eggs.

'We need to hide, Echo,' whispered Horace urgently, pulling her away. 'It's a female and we do *not* want to wake her.'

But Echo couldn't tear herself away from watching the dragon, her eyes wide and her stomach fizzing with a mixture of fear and excitement. She finally ducked back into the tunnel, after quickly scanning the mountain of gold for any sign of the cutlass. She took a deep breath, taking in the smell of sulphur and a hint of peppermint.

'Isn't it wonderful, Horace?' she said. 'I didn't quite believe we would really see a dragon, but—'

'We have to get out of here,' Horace hissed. 'That dragon will eat us as a snack, Echo! Don't you know how many explorers have tried to plunder dragons' lairs and never returned? And this one's a nesting female, which is at least ten times worse!'

'I'm not leaving until I've got the cutlass,' said Echo. 'We've come this far. We can't just bail out now. Perhaps I can creep in without her noticing somehow.' But even Echo knew this would never work. There was simply too much gold. She'd never find the cutlass before the dragon woke up.

Echo was stirred out of her thoughts by Gilbert, who scrambled up to Echo's shoulder and butted her cheek with his snout as if to say, *Talk to her.*

'What? I don't know how,' whispered Echo.

'What are you on about?' whispered back Horace.

'I'm talking to Gilbert.'

Horace folded his arms. 'This isn't time for a chat. We need to find the way out. This is too dangerous – even you have to admit it.'

Echo shook her head. 'We didn't get stranded at Shark's Fin Peak, kidnapped by Old Gus and separated from the Black Sky Wolves just to leave now. What about the cutlass? We can't just let the others find it. We're sky pirates – or at least I am.'

Horace folded his arms. 'I don't know what you're trying to prove, Echo.'

'I'm just trying to—'

Behind them, the click of high heels on stone rang out. 'Well, what do we have here?' The familiar voice made Echo's skin crawl and she whipped round in horror.

There before her, green-nailed hands on hips, stood Miranda Vossberg.

CHAPTER TWENTY-NINE

Before Echo could reach for *Stinger*, Miranda had her own cutlass at Horace's throat. 'Don't even try it,' she snarled. 'Out, now.' She marched Echo and Horace through yet another maze of tunnels, these ones wide and scorch-marked and covered with the glow jars Miranda had bought in Amaranth Point.

They climbed over collapsed rocks, round clusters of razor-sharp stalagmites and waded through pools of murky reddish water, until finally the three of them emerged, blinking, into daylight as the tunnel surfaced at the rim of the volcano crater.

Miranda led them to a rock that arched into the sky like a giant rib bone on the volcano's upper slope. She tossed Echo a rope. 'Bind his hands.'

'What?'

'You heard me. And do it tightly. I'm not stupid.'

Echo looked from Miranda's vicious smile to Horace's terrified face.

'Quickly,' snapped Miranda. 'Or I can just kill him now.'

Horace put his hands out in front of him, wrists together, and Echo bound them with the rope.

'Excellent.' Miranda stepped towards Echo with another rope.

'W . . . what do you want me to do?' asked Echo.

Miranda laughed cruelly. 'Oh, just hang around here and be delicious,' she said. 'Dragons like young flesh.'

'But . . . but you can't!' Echo squirmed, as Miranda bound her hands behind her back. 'You can't just leave us here to be eaten!'

'I think you'll find I can,' said Miranda, with a smirk. 'It will be an honourable end. I'll make sure your sacrifice is remembered when I am queen of all the seven skies.'

She shoved Echo and Horace towards the slender, rib-shaped rock and ran their ropes round it so they were tied back to back. 'This looks like the perfect spot. It'll take a good few gulps to get rid of you, which gives me time to retrieve the cutlass. Now, where are those marshmallows?'

'Marshmallows?' Echo whispered to Horace.

Horace shook his head sorrowfully. 'Dragons have a sweet tooth,' he whispered. 'Old Gus brought a whole crate of chocolate fudge cake.'

Echo glanced over at where her knapsack lay discarded in the dirt, wishing they hadn't toasted all the marshmallows she'd collected in the marshes. Perhaps they could have used them to pacify the dragon somehow. She swallowed down her fear. Before they were burned to a crisp, that was.

Miranda took out a paper bag from her pocket and scattered a few marshmallows near Echo's and Horace's feet before stalking back towards the entrance to the lava tube, leaving a trail of the pink sweets behind her.

As she turned away, Echo felt Gilbert scuttle out of her collar and run down her back. She twisted as far as she could and looked over her shoulder. 'What are you doing?' she hissed.

But Gilbert didn't answer. Instead, he grabbed at the knot with his jaws, braced all four feet on Echo's back and shook the rope as hard as he could. Echo's heart leaped.

Echo twisted her hands and felt the binding round her wrists loosen. 'That's it,' she said. 'A little more.'

Gilbert strained his little scaly body until finally the rope slipped and Echo pulled her hands free. She glanced over at Miranda, who was nearly at the entrance to the tunnel. Anger flooded through Echo in a wave. She wouldn't let Miranda get the Cutlass of Calinthe. If anyone deserved it, it was Lil. Lil would use it to do the right thing.

Echo drew *Stinger* from her boot with a *swish* and felt a low thrum of energy vibrate up her arm.

'Stop!' she shouted.

Miranda turned, a look of surprise on her face. 'How did you ...' She caught sight of Echo's sword and laughed. 'Still want to fight me? Didn't you learn your lesson last time?'

'I'm not going to let you get that cutlass,' said Echo, trying to stop her voice from shaking. She advanced again. 'If anyone should have it, it's my mother, Lil. She'd use it to do the right thing.'

'The right thing!' Miranda's voice dripped with sarcasm. 'Who cares about that? I'm the only one who can lead the sky pirates to victory. Under my command, we'll rule the world!'

'A true sky pirate wouldn't want to rule the world,' said Echo. 'A true sky pirate would fight for good.'

'What would you know about being a sky pirate? You're just a child.' Miranda drew her cutlass and stalked towards Echo.

Echo's heart raced, but she stood her ground and tightened her grip on *Stinger*, who vibrated in her hand. 'I know that a true sky pirate would never attack a defenceless, sleeping creature,' she said. 'A true sky pirate would be clever enough to get the gold without hurting anybody.'

For a moment, Miranda's brow creased in a frown, then she recovered herself. 'It's just a dragon,' she said, with a forced laugh. 'A beast.' Her voice grew stronger. 'A dangerous beast that would wreak havoc on anyone who came close to it. I'm doing the world a favour – they're just too stupid to see it.'

'No,' said Echo, feeling the heat rise in her cheeks. Even if she couldn't stop Miranda from getting the cutlass, she had to convince her to spare the dragon. 'If you would just take the time to understand. She's a mother. She's protecting her eggs!'

Miranda's eyes sparkled. 'Eggs? Well, I can add those to my collection along with the cutlass. They'll fetch a pretty penny at Amaranth Point!' She shrugged one green, leather-clad shoulder. 'If you show me where they are, I'll cut the Black Sky Wolves half.'

'No way,' said Echo. 'Helping you is the last thing I'd do.'

'In that case, I'll just have to get rid of you here and now.' Miranda swished her cutlass and advanced on Echo, baring her teeth in a ferocious grin. 'Do you really think I'm scared of a child?' She ran at Echo, her cutlass raised.

Echo ducked as the blade swished over her head and crashed into a clump of thorny bushes. She rolled clear, landing in the red dirt, then jumped to her feet, *Stinger* held out in front of her, ready to fight.

Miranda attacked again and Echo blocked her blow with a *clang*. The force of the blow reverberated up Echo's arm, making her wince, but she held steady and forced Miranda backwards.

Miranda reached into her belt and drew out the bullwhip with her other hand, flicking it with a crack that sent up clouds of rust-coloured dirt.

Echo coughed and covered her face as the thick dust choked her.

Miranda saw her chance and flicked the whip again. The leathery coils snaked towards Echo, wrapped round *Stinger* and wrenched it out of Echo's hand, flinging it into the undergrowth.

'No!' Echo staggered backwards, weaponless. She tripped on a gnarled root and went tumbling to the ground. Miranda was almost upon her, her teeth bared in a horrible smile.

'Echo, look out!' Horace shouted, as Echo staggered to her feet.

Miranda flicked the whip with a crack. The coils wrapped round Echo until her arms were pinned to her sides and she was completely helpless.

'Nice try,' Miranda panted. 'But you won't defeat me.'

She marched Echo back over to where Horace was tied, his face ghost-white and eyes wide, removed the whip and retied Echo's hands.

'I'll tie it extra tightly this time.' She gave the rope a yank that made Echo yelp as pain shot through her wrists. 'You won't be getting out of that until you're ripped out in a dragon's jaws.'

Miranda stormed back to the entrance of the lava tube, and disappeared into the darkness, cutlass glinting, leaving Echo and Horace tied helplessly to the rock and a faint scent of peppermint in the air.

CHAPTER THIRTY

Horace shook his head sorrowfully as he and Echo stood back to back, tied tightly to the rock. 'You should have just waited until she'd gone. We could have run away!' he said.

'Sky pirates don't run away.' Echo's hands tingled as the ropes bit into her wrists and she wriggled uselessly against them. She looked for Gilbert, who had disappeared under a thorn bush during Echo's fight with Miranda. 'Gilbert, where are you?'

She saw a flash of yellow as the little lizard scuttled out of the undergrowth and ran up Echo's leg. But, however hard he tried, Miranda really had tied them up securely this time. After struggling for several minutes, the little lizard flopped, exhausted, into the red dirt, and Echo was still bound as tight as ever. Her arms ached where they had been forced unnaturally behind her back. She glanced around in desperation. *Stinger* still lay where it had landed in the bushes, out of reach and far too heavy for Gilbert to manage. There really was no way out this time.

'We could have escaped,' continued Horace. 'We could have waited for Lil and the others to arrive.'

Echo squinted into the distance. Six airships were dotted round Mount Enoc. *Anaconda* was moored close to the volcano's mouth. The yellow-sailed ship circled above the river. Even the *Purple People Eater*, its balloons patched with grimy sailcloth, and *Obsidian*, still soot-stained but functioning, had arrived. But the *Scarlet Margaret* was nowhere to be seen.

Perhaps Lil never got my message at all, Echo thought despondently. *Or perhaps she decided not to come.*

Echo shook herself. No, Lil was her mother. There was no way she would leave Echo here, with dragons and danger and six rival sky-pirate clans! Something must have held them up. In the meantime, there had to be something Echo could do to stop Miranda.

'We have to get that cutlass,' she said. 'Can you see anything that would help us?'

'Really, Echo? Who *cares* about the cutlass when we're about to get eaten by a dragon!'

'I care. And you will too once Miranda's in charge of the seven skies. She's dangerous, Horace.'

'I think there's more we need to be worrying about . . .' Horace trailed off.

'What is it?' Echo strained to look at him and the entrance to the caves over her shoulder. 'What can you see?'

'Listen!'

Echo froze. She could hear footsteps. No, she could *feel* footsteps. Footsteps so large and heavy that they shook the very mountain they were standing on.

The footsteps grew louder. There was a deep rumble that seemed to vibrate through Echo's bones and the great, gleaming red dragon came lumbering out of the volcano.

The dragon sniffed and daintily licked up a marshmallow with her long, forked tongue. Smoke spiralled from her nostrils and she regarded them unblinkingly with catlike amber eyes.

'W . . . what should we do?' said Echo. It had been one thing looking at the sleeping dragon and imagining taking a piece of its gold, but seeing her up close, awake and dangerous, was quite another.

'I don't know!' whimpered Horace. 'Close our eyes and prepare to die?'

The dragon took another pace forward, lashing her muscular tail from side to side with a *whump whump*.

'Is that good?' Echo asked. 'That she's wagging her tail?'

Horace shook his head vigorously. 'No. It's bad. Very bad . . . Oh no!'

'What now?' Echo's heart stilled as she saw the little golden-scaled figure of Gilbert scuttling across the rocks straight towards the dragon.

'Gilbert, no!' she hissed. Gilbert paused and cocked his head towards her, then turned back and continued to run right up to the dragon's snout.

Echo's heart almost stopped beating entirely as the dragon's nostrils flared and she stared at Gilbert with her amber eyes. Echo grabbed Horace's hand and squeezed it tight as Gilbert crept closer.

'What is he doing?' whispered Horace.

'I don't know!' Sweat prickled on Echo's forehead. She strained uselessly at her bonds. If only she could break free and pluck him out of harm's way!

The dragon opened her jaws in a wide-mouthed yawn and dropped her snout so that she was nose to nose with Gilbert. Echo held her breath as Gilbert raised his crest and bowed his head low.

What was he doing? She clenched her jaw in trepidation as he continued to bob his head.

The dragon watched in silence, before raising her own crest in response. Echo's mouth dropped open. 'I think he ... he's talking to her,' she murmured.

'Talking to ... to a dragon?'

'Yes! That's what he said to me before. That we should talk to her.'

Horace shook his head in disbelief. 'I suppose dragons and lizards are related, zoologically speaking,' he said. 'But still, it seems implausible that—'

'Look!'

The dragon bobbed her head in turn and blew smoky breath over Gilbert, before butting him, ever so gently, with her snout.

Echo and Horace both broke into huge grins.

'Is . . . is she friendly?' asked Horace. 'I can't believe it.'

'Shh!' Echo pointed at Gilbert, who was racing back across the rocks towards them. When he reached them, he tugged at Echo's boot laces and turned back to the dragon as if to say, *Come on*.

Echo's eyes widened in terror as the dragon lumbered towards them, her tail still swishing this way and that. She could feel Horace shaking behind her.

The dragon lowered her huge head and looked Echo right in the eye. Then she opened her jaws, revealing rows of razor-sharp teeth, each one as big as Echo's hand.

Echo gasped in horror. This was it. This was how it was all going to end. She clutched Horace's hand and squeezed her eyes tightly shut.

CHAPTER THIRTY-ONE

To Echo's surprise, all she felt was a soft nudge to her belly, followed by the slackening of her ropes as they slipped off and fell to the dusty ground. When she opened her eyes again, she was amazed to see the dragon, very gently, turning to Horace and slicing through the ropes that bound him with her teeth.

Horace looked down at himself, then at Echo in amazement. 'We're . . . we're free,' he said.

The dragon bobbed her head.

'Can she understand us?' he said, his eyes wide. 'She can't . . . can she?'

'I don't see why not,' said Echo, still not quite believing this turn of events. 'Gilbert can, so why shouldn't a dragon?'

She turned to the dragon and gave a nervous curtsy. 'You should go,' she said. 'It isn't safe for you here. Miranda will kill you if she gets the chance . . .' She trailed off as the dragon made a strange gagging, hiccuping sound.

'What's she doing?' Echo asked.

'I've got absolutely no idea,' said Horace.

'You're the dragon expert!'

'Well, she looks like . . . like one of the professor's cats when they bring up a furball.'

'What?'

'I think she's going to be sick!' Horace paled and took several paces backwards.

The dragon's cheeks bulged and, with a rumble, she spat out one of her eggs, which lay gleaming red in the dust.

'She must know Miranda's up to no good,' Echo whispered.

Horace nodded. 'Mountain dragons always keep their eggs close to their side, even when they're hunting,' he said. 'Some varieties have special pouches in their throat to keep their eggs safe.'

The dragon gagged again and brought up a second egg, this one a brilliant emerald green. Then, with a final throaty groan, she spat out a golden egg, before nudging all three towards Echo and Horace with her snout.

'You want us to protect them?' asked Echo, turning to the dragon.

The dragon bobbed her head again, then cocked it to one side, as if listening.

Gilbert cocked his head too, then his scales flashed red for danger.

'What is it?' Echo said. Then she heard it. The distant stomp of boots and the shouts of rough sky-pirate voices were ringing faintly through the lava tubes. There were lots of them, and they were getting louder.

The dragon nudged the eggs towards Echo and Horace again.

'We'll look after them,' Echo said. 'I promise.' As the footsteps and shouts grew louder, she and Horace quickly rolled the dragon eggs, each as big as a watermelon, into the bushes and hid alongside them.

'Here it is!'

Echo turned to see Miranda emerging from the tunnel, a victorious smile on her face.

The dragon turned, slow as a sky galleon, towards the cave entrance, her huge red tail lashing from side to side.

Behind Miranda, a gaggle of sky pirates in all the varied colours of the Seven Skies flooded out of the tunnels, their arms and pockets overflowing with gold and jewels. Echo spotted a sad-looking Grub and her heart clenched with guilt at how she'd tricked him with the imaginary aethernet.

Miranda drew a glittering gold cutlass from her belt and raised it above her head. At this, all the sky pirates dropped down to their knees behind her. Among them, Echo saw sky pirates of every clan. Steel-eyed Seth in his yellow jerkin, his mechanical eye firmly focused on the gleaming blade. Rashmi the Ruthless, her thick black plait flung over one purple-clad

shoulder. Even Old Gus, his pockets brimming with pearls, was bowing down to Miranda.

It was the Cutlass of Calinthe, Echo realized in horror. She had failed. Miranda had found it, and now all the sky-pirate clans were under her command.

'I am the queen of the seven skies!' shouted Miranda. 'And I command you all to kill that dragon!'

Miranda raised her flintlock and fired a volley of shots at the dragon.

The other sky pirates whooped and cheered and ran forward in a terrifying pack, teeth bared, cutlasses held high, swarming all over the crater and surrounding the dragon.

There was a red flash of flame as the dragon roared, shooting fire across the volcano crater.

Echo gasped and shrank back further into the bushes as the dragon's wings beat with a huge *whump whump* and she soared into the air, pressing the wild grass flat with the downdraught of her wings. She roared with rage, a deafening sound that rumbled all round the canyon.

Echo watched in horror as Old Gus led a group of blue-clad Thunder Sharks forward, some wielding cutlasses, others firing pistols.

The dragon screeched and sent a cascade of orange flame down on to them. Old Gus screamed as he was blown into the air, the seat of his breeches aflame. He tumbled down the volcano, finally landing in the river with a huge hiss of steam.

The dragon blasted another torrent of flame that licked up the rib-shaped rock and scorched the edges of the bushes Echo and Horace were hidden in.

'We have to get out of here,' whispered Horace.

'But we need to help her,' Echo hissed back.

Horace shook his head. 'No, we need to take these somewhere safe,' he said, gesturing to the three eggs hidden in the bushes.

Echo nodded. Horace was right. If they stayed where they were, they'd end up char-grilled, even if the dragon wasn't aiming at them. She turned and stuffed two of the eggs into her knapsack. Horace packed the last one into his satchel.

'Echo!' Echo jerked her head up to see Grub, his face pinched with fear, staggering down the slope towards them. 'What are you doing here? Are those ... ?' He pointed a shaking finger at the dragon eggs.

'You can't have them,' she said, brandishing *Stinger* and taking a step forward.

'I ... I don't want them,' said Grub, flinging both hands in the air. 'I didn't want any of this.' He flinched as gunshot flared up on the volcano's rim.

Echo took in his terrified face. 'Over here,' she said, scrambling down the volcano slope, out of sight of the pirates, who were all either firing their guns and whooping, or cowering from the dragon's flames. They found another clump of bushes to hide in and took cover beneath the thorny foliage.

'Are you okay?' asked Echo.

Grub shook his head, his shoulders quivering. 'I've always wanted to see a real dragon,' he said. 'It makes me sick to see them attacking it like that. Old Gus said he'd have me thrown in the shark tank if I didn't go down there!'

There was a faint yell from below and Echo peeked down to the river to see a somewhat singed Old Gus doggy-paddling to the riverbank and dragging himself out.

Grub looked too and swallowed. 'I'd better get back,' he said.

'Are you sure?' Echo said. 'You could come with us. Help us save these eggs.'

Grub licked his lips and paused for a moment, then finally shook his head. 'I can't,' he said sadly. 'Here, have your aethernet back, in case it comes in handy.' He carefully pulled the imaginary net out of his pocket and passed it to Echo.

'Thanks,' she said softly, heat flushing her cheeks.

'Bye then.' Grub raced back up the volcano slope. Above them, there was the buzz of airship engines, and Echo looked up to see all six of the sky-pirate ships closing in on the dragon. There was the boom of a cannon and something flew past them and crashed into the volcano in a burst of orange flame.

The dragon spun this way and that, her tail lashing the air, but there were too many ships and too many cannons firing.

'No!' Echo shouted in horror as she looked back to see Miranda, pistol in hand, silhouetted on the volcano's rim. Echo's hand instinctively reached for *Stinger*, but, before she had time to react, the pirate captain raised her flintlock pistol to the sky, aiming it directly at the dragon's soft underbelly.

BANG!

The whole world seemed to slow as, with a terrible, heart-rending screech, the dragon fell out of the sky like a glittering red stone and plummeted into the river far, far below.

CHAPTER THIRTY-TWO

The world seemed to spin round her as Echo stared in despair at the river below. Steam billowed from its surface, and the impact of the dragon's fall sent waves surging outwards and up the riverbanks. But the dragon didn't emerge and, after several moments, the truth hit Echo.

'They killed her!' She turned to Horace in disbelief.

From the volcano's crater, there were jubilant cheers and whoops from the other sky-pirate clans. A sick feeling roiled in Echo's stomach as she and Horace crouched, frozen in the bushes, the two dragon eggs weighing heavy in her bag.

'I can't believe it,' said Horace, his face white.

'Moor the ships! Load them with gold!' Miranda yelled from behind them. 'Then get back down there and clear the cave out. Every one of you!'

There were cries of, 'Yes, my queen!' and, 'Certainly, boss!' as the six ships buzzed lower and landed on Mount Enoc's crater.

'How could they?' Echo's sorrow turned to fury and she reached for *Stinger*. 'They don't deserve that gold. Not a single doubloon of it. I'll show them.'

'No, Echo.' Horace stood in front of her. 'You can't fight all of them.'

'But we *should* have fought. We could have stopped them.' Regret flooded through Echo's veins and she felt tears build behind her eyes. She sniffed and shoved *Stinger* back in her boot.

'It's not your fault.' Horace shook his head. 'We would have just got ourselves captured. Or killed.' He scrubbed his eyes on the back of his sleeve and peered down at the river below. 'Perhaps she's just injured. Maybe we can go down there and help her.'

They scrambled a few metres down the slope and stood for several minutes, staring at the rushing water. But there was not even a glimmer of red scales.

'I think she's really gone,' said Echo.

Horace nodded and let out a big sob.

The tears that had been building finally slipped down Echo's face. 'We've failed,' she sobbed. 'Miranda has the cutlass and the dragon is dead! Some sky pirate I am.'

Horace flung his arms round her and, for several moments, they both just stood and wept. Gilbert scuttled up on to Echo's shoulder, his scales blue-violet with sorrow, and rubbed her cheek.

'We did our best, Echo,' Horace said softly, as they drew apart.

'I suppose.' Echo bowed her head and her eye alighted on her knapsack. 'At least they didn't get her eggs,' she said. She hefted the knapsack on to her shoulder, then froze at the sound of propellers.

'Oh no!' Horace paled. 'Not more sky pirates?' He ducked behind a rock, pulling Echo and Gilbert with him.

'More?' Echo frowned. But all six of the rival clans were here already. Could it possibly be . . . ? No, it didn't sound like the *Scarlet Margaret*. She peeked out in trepidation and felt her whole body sag in relief at the sight of *Cloudcatcher* and Lil, zooming towards them.

For a moment, Echo felt a flicker of uncertainty as Lil spotted them and brought *Cloudcatcher* down in a clearing between the bushes, sending clouds of red dust up into the air. Was Lil really here for her? Or was she after the dragon's gold, like all the others?

But, as Lil pushed her flying goggles up on to her forehead and raced over to them, Echo saw the relief and love in Lil's face and she knew the answer.

'Echo! Horace!' Lil's voice shook.

'Mother! You found me!'

'Oh, Echo, of course I did!' Lil flung herself at Echo and hugged her tight.

Echo buried her head in Lil's leather jerkin and breathed in her familiar smell of cinnamon and gunpowder. She finally looked up. 'They killed the dragon.'

'So I saw,' said Lil grimly. She stood back from Echo and looked her up and down. 'Are you all right though?'

Echo nodded. 'We're fine.' She glanced over at the little gyrocopter and frowned. 'You got *Cloudcatcher* back. But . . . but how?'

'There's no time for that.' Lil pointed up at *Anaconda* and the other ships. 'There are too many other pirate crews around. We need to get out of here. Come on.'

She hurried Echo and Horace into *Cloudcatcher* and steered the little craft across the canyon walls and down to a valley where the *Scarlet Margaret* was moored.

When they'd got onboard and Bulkhead had hauled in the anchor, Lil swung the *Scarlet Margaret* round and they powered upwards until they were beyond the clouds. Finally, Lil took a breath and turned to look at Echo.

'What happened to you?' she said. 'I was frantic with worry. After the alliance meeting, I checked in on you both at breakfast time and you were gone!'

Echo nodded, her face burning, and explained how they'd taken *Cloudcatcher* to Shark's Fin Peak.

Lil nodded. 'Of course, we thought that was what you must have done when we found out *Cloudcatcher* was missing. Then, when we went back to Shark's Fin Peak, we spotted it in that crevasse and we thought ... I thought ...' Lil trailed off, her voice breaking.

'But we knew yer must be okay, Echo,' said Bulkhead, from the ship's wheel. 'We hauled up *Cloudcatcher* and you two were nowhere to be seen, so we figured you must have got away somewhere.'

Lil nodded and scrubbed her eyes with her sleeve. 'So we set a course for the Aqualiber Vaults to try to catch up with the Thunder Sharks.'

'Narrowly missing being cannon fodder,' added Slingshot, with a lopsided grin.

'You put yourself in danger, Echo,' said Lil, fixing Echo with a steely glare. 'You disobeyed your captain's orders.'

Echo felt her cheeks burn. 'I'm sorry,' she said.

Lil's frown dissolved and she hugged Echo again. 'I suppose there's no real harm done,' she said. 'You're both back and safe, and that's the important thing. Now, let's get as far away from here as possible before Viper Voss returns.'

Viper Voss! Echo thought back to the conversation she'd overheard all those nights ago on the *Scarlet Margaret*. Miranda Vossberg was the one Bulkhead had been warning Lil about.

Echo couldn't quite meet Lil's eye. 'She has the cutlass,' she mumbled.

'I know,' said Lil, patting Echo's hand. 'Nothing to be done about it now though. For the moment, we get out of the Dragonlands and as far from the others as we can.'

'I suppose.' Echo slumped down on the gunwale and finally heaved her bulging knapsack down off her back.

Spud eyed it with a grin. 'What yer got in there?'

Echo opened it, gazing sadly at the two dragon eggs she had carried. 'We need to work out what to do with these.'

Lil's eyes widened as Horace opened his satchel too, revealing the third egg. 'Those'll fetch a pretty penny. They're worth more than any gold haul!'

'No, we can't keep them.' Echo shook her head. 'We made a promise,' she said. 'To the dragon.'

'Talking to dragons?' Lil arched an eyebrow. 'I should know by now never to be surprised by you, Echo. What do you need to do?'

Echo grinned, an idea forming in her mind. 'Horace and I need to take *Cloudcatcher*. But we'll bring her back safe this time. I promise.'

CHAPTER THIRTY-THREE

'Are you sure this is a good idea?' asked Lil, her brow creased with worry, as Echo and Horace climbed into *Cloudcatcher*. 'You know what happened last time you flew off on your own.'

'We'll be fine,' said Echo, fastening her harness. 'You don't need to worry, Mother. I promise.'

Lil shook her head. 'And you're sure you know the way?'

'Can't miss it,' said Echo, focusing on the smoking crater of Mount Vaal at the other end of the canyon. 'We'll come straight back.'

'I think these are securely attached!' Bulkhead shouted up from where he was working beneath *Cloudcatcher*. 'Just pull on this thread here and that'll release the net.'

He passed Horace the whisper-fine aethernet thread and stepped back as Echo fired up the engines. With a whirr, the propeller began to spin and *Cloudcatcher* lifted slowly into the air.

'We'll meet you back here!' shouted Lil, above the buzz of the engines. 'In the meantime, we'll head back to the dragon's lair to see what treasure can be salvaged.'

'Once the others have gone,' added Bulkhead.

Lil nodded. 'It's too dangerous to take on the six other sky-pirate clans as one, but perhaps they'll leave something behind.'

'Okay.' For a moment, Echo's heart was torn. The Black Sky Wolves' coffers really were empty now. Perhaps they should keep just one of the dragon eggs to sell. It would solve all their money problems after all. She glanced at the three eggs, gleaming red, green and gold as they dangled in the aethernet that hung beneath *Cloudcatcher*. Then she caught Horace's eye and flushed. No. She'd made a promise to the dragon. They both had. And they were going to keep it.

'Be careful!' shouted Lil.

'I will!' Echo yelled back, and she brought *Cloudcatcher* higher, past Slingshot, who saluted from the crow's nest, and up into the air.

As they left Mount Enoc behind, Echo took a last glimpse over her shoulder. All six of the other airships were moored close to the entrance to the dragon's lair. Around them, sky pirates swarmed all over the mountain, carrying armfuls of gold back to their ships, while Miranda stood in the centre of it all, the Cutlass of Calinthe glinting at her hip.

Echo's belly knotted with regret and she tightened her grip on *Cloudcatcher*'s controls. Those pirates didn't deserve any of it. She turned the gyrocopter away and pointed its nose in the direction of Mount Vaal.

Mount Vaal was wreathed in murky clouds, and the further north they flew up the canyon, the darker the sky grew. Soon rain was falling on them, running in rivulets down Echo's nose and washing the red dust from her skin. As they approached the volcano, the clouds crackled around them and there was a low rumble of thunder.

'Look.' Horace pointed into the crater, his blond hair plastered to his face.

Echo blinked the rain out of her eyes and followed his gaze, careful to keep *Cloudcatcher* steady, and felt her breath catch as she saw the red glow of molten lava bubbling and spitting in the volcano's mouth.

'Do you really think this is going to work?' Horace asked.

'Miranda told me dragons were forged in flame,' said Echo, thinking back to her first day onboard *Anaconda*. It seemed like a lifetime ago. 'The eggs hatch in the heat of their mother's fiery breath.'

'And a dragon's breath is as hot as a volcano,' agreed Horace.

'Well, here goes.' Echo braced herself. 'On three, okay?' She steered *Cloudcatcher* right over the volcano cone, squinting as the plumes of smoke surrounded them.

'One . . . two . . . three!'

Horace wrestled with the aethernet threads as Echo battled with the controls. Sparks and smut flew all around them, turning to sludge as they hit their wet skin.

Echo spat ash from her mouth and wiped grey water from her goggles. 'Have you done it?'

'It's got tangled somehow!' Horace shouted.

'Now?'

Horace shook his head. 'It's stuck!'

Cloudcatcher bucked on the currents of hot air and a bolt of lightning fizzed through the sky. Echo felt a thrum of energy from *Stinger*. Of course!

'Hold these!' she shouted, swivelling the controls over.

She drew *Stinger* from her boot, feeling the familiar warmth spread up her arm with a *zing*. She reached down, rain soaking her back, and swiped at the net with her sword.

And, with a *swish*, Echo sliced through the aethernet and the three eggs, red, green and gold, went tumbling through the air and into Mount Vaal's hungry red-glowing mouth.

'Has it worked?' Echo steered *Cloudcatcher* out of the fiery winds of Mount Vaal and dropped into a holding pattern once they were a safe distance away. 'Can you see anything?'

'Not yet.' Horace put the spyglass to his eye and squinted through the rain.

Gilbert climbed up on to Echo's head and peered out too, his crest raised in anticipation.

'How long will it take them to hatch?'

'I don't know!'

Echo clenched her fists on the controls in frustration. It had to work! Otherwise this had all been a huge waste of time. Fear washed over her. They could have sold the eggs. The Black Sky Wolves would never have had to worry about money again. Had it all been for nothing?

Horace lowered the spyglass. 'It was a risk, Echo,' he said. 'We didn't know for a fact they'd hatch in the volcano.'

'But you said volcanoes are as hot as dragon's breath.'

'Maybe I was wrong,' said Horace.

'Shall we wait a little longer?' asked Echo forlornly. A vision of the dragon's elegant ruby-red body crashing so heavily into the water flashed back before her eyes and sadness settled in her stomach. 'It has to work,' she whispered.

'We tried, Echo,' said Horace. 'We did our best.'

'I suppose.' Echo pushed the wet hair out of her eyes, her heart heavy with disappointment. 'We should go back to the others.' She pulled on the handles and began to wheel *Cloudcatcher* round

'Echo, wait!' Horace grabbed her arm. 'I thought I saw ... Yes!'

'What?' Echo followed Horace's gaze and her heart soared with relief as three baby dragons, one

red, one green and one gold, burst out of the volcano, roaring and spitting flames.

CHAPTER THIRTY-FOUR

It was much later, when the sun was just a scarlet flare on the horizon, that Echo landed *Cloudcatcher* back on the deck of the *Scarlet Margaret* to the cheers of the waiting crew. Echo took in their expectant faces.

'Well?' said Lil. 'Did you manage it?'

Echo nodded, unable to speak for a moment.

'All three of them flew,' said Horace. 'We saw them. It was spectacular!'

'Well done.' Lil flushed with pride. 'I'm proud of you both. We all are, aren't we?'

Another cheer went up from the rest of the crew, and Bulkhead lifted Echo on to his shoulders. Horace let out a squeal as he was hoisted into the air by Slingshot and Beti.

'You're a true Black Sky Wolf, Echo,' said Lil. 'You fought for good.'

Echo grinned from ear to ear as the Black Sky Wolves

marched down to the main deck, where Spud and Skillet had arranged the tables in a ring, set with candles and tankards of grog.

She scrambled down from Bulkhead's shoulders and took her place at the table between Horace and Lil.

'I'd like to raise a toast,' said Lil. 'To being a true sky pirate. To fighting for good.'

'And to dragons,' said Echo and Horace at the same time.

Gilbert chirruped in agreement from Echo's shoulder.

'And to dragons.' Lil raised her tankard.

'TO DRAGONS!' The cheer went round the table as everyone clinked their glasses together.

In the flickering warmth of the candle glow, they settled down to eat. 'I'm afraid it's only grilled starfish and seaweed crackers tonight,' said Spud. 'That's all we have left from the store. There's nothing much to forage around here.'

Echo's grin slipped for a moment. No food left! What would they do? She turned to Lil. 'We didn't get any of the gold, did we?'

Lil shook her head. 'No. They'd cleared it all out by the time we got back into the caves.'

'I'm sorry.' Echo's heart filled with guilt and she twisted her hands together. 'It's my fault. I shouldn't have—'

'You did the right thing,' said Lil. 'That's what a true sky pirate does.' She set down her fork and put an arm round Echo. 'There'll always be more treasure to find. And, in the meantime, starfish and seaweed with the daughter I love is just fine by me.'

Echo felt her cheeks flush with pride and she flung both her arms round Lil and buried her head in her leather jerkin.

Then she swallowed and pulled back. 'But what about the Cutlass of Calinthe?'

Lil nodded grimly. 'There's no changing things. Miranda has it, which makes her the leader of the seven skies.'

'Does she lead us?'

Lil snorted, almost spitting her grog across the table. 'No. She does not.'

'But what will we do. Now the other six clans are all one?'

'I won't lie,' said Lil. 'Things are going to be a lot more dangerous with Miranda in charge. I really don't know what the future holds. But we'll manage,' she said. 'We always do. We're the Black Sky Wolves after all.'

Echo nodded.

'Wait, that reminds me.' Lil got up and marched over to the captain's quarters, returning with something held behind her back. 'The crew and I decided you'd earned this.' She brought out a hatbox and opened it to reveal an indigo wool tricorne.

Echo's heart swelled with pride. Then she frowned. 'But . . . but where did you get a tricorne in the Dragonlands?'

'I bought it a long time ago, Echo,' said

Lil. 'I knew you'd earn it one day. It was just a question of when.'

Echo grinned from ear to ear as Lil placed the stiff woollen hat on to her curls.

It fitted perfectly.

'So,' Echo said shyly to Flora later, as she speared a juicy, chargrilled starfish with her fork, 'am I a princess or a pirate now?'

'Definitely a pirate,' said Flora, with a smile.

'Definitely,' agreed Horace.

'Through and through,' said Lil.

As the sky dimmed to violet, Echo couldn't help grinning from her place at the pot wash where she was washing up plates. She looked round the ship, taking in the crew's smiling faces. Lil was busy studying the sky charts, the cream plume on her tricorne bobbing as she spoke to Bulkhead, who frowned in concentration. Spud and Beti sloshed soapy water over the decks with some help from Slingshot, every now and then breaking out into a mock swordfight with their mops. Flora and Horace had their heads together as they packed away the tables. And somewhere, out there in the Dragonlands, the three baby dragons were flying, wild and free as they should be, singing the songs of the seven skies and the story of how they'd been forged in fire.

Miranda might have the Cutlass of Calinthe, and Echo hadn't brought back a single sovereign of the dragon's gold, but she was happy, and she belonged.

She was a sky pirate.

And, for the moment, that was quite enough.

ACKNOWLEDGEMENTS

I would like to give a hearty Sky Pirate thank you to the following people:

Thérèse Coen, my superstar of an agent, who supported Echo and her motley crew from the very start.

My brilliant editors, Lucy Rogers and Amina Youssef, who steered the good ship Sky Pirates in the right direction and helped me make this book even better than I'd imagined it could be.

Mark Chambers, for his fantastic illustrations, Jesse Green for her design chops, Jane Tait for her meticulous wordsmithery and all the rest of the team at Simon & Schuster for their enthusiasm and all-round fabulousness.

Team Swag, Tania and Sarah for the cheerleading and handholding behind the scenes. Ellie, Hannah and Jane for the Zoom tomfoolery and helping to keep me sane during the pandemic.

Freddie and George for their boundless enthusiasm and for asking me at least a million times, 'Have you finished it yet?' Yes, boys, I have!

And finally, Rik, for the (many) cups of tea and keeping the boys out of my hair when I needed it. I couldn't have done this without you.

Recipe for
Marshamallama Milkshakes

Ingredients:

200ml marshmallama milk (regular dairy or
alternative milk can also be used if you don't have
a marshmallama to hand)
A handful of mini pink marshmallows
(plus a few to decorate)
1 scoop vanilla ice cream

Method:

Put all the ingredients in a blender and whizz
until smooth.
Decorate the top with some more marshmallows.
Drink on adventures.

SKY PIRATES QUIZ!

1 How many dragon eggs do Echo and Horace find?

    a) Five

    b) Three

    c) One

2 What is inside the treasure chest that Echo digs up?

    a) A disgruntled octopus

    b) Gold doubloons

    c) A ruby necklace

3 Complete the clue: 'To find the way to dragon caves, seek knowledge underneath the . . .'

    a) . . . sofa cushions

    b) . . . waves

    c) . . . stairs

4 What is the name of the Thunder Sharks' airship?

    a) Jaws

    b) Diamond

    c) Obsidian

5 What form of transport does Gerund, the librarian, use?

    a) Jetpack
    b) Tricycle
    c) Roller skates

6 What is the name of Echo's cutlass?

    a) Stinger
    b) Slasher
    c) Spike

7 What colour is the mist in the Mallow Marshes?

    a) Pink
    b) Purple
    c) Blue

8 What do Echo and Horace find to eat in Tarakona Canyon?

    a) Pickled squibnuts
    b) Dragon fruit
    c) Apples

TURN TO THE NEXT PAGE FOR THE ANSWERS!

QUIZ ANSWERS:

1) B, 2) A, 3) B, 4) C, 5) B, 6) A, 7) A, 8) B

How many did you get right?

1-2 There's a way to go before you're ready to sail the seven skies. Perhaps you're better off on land!

3-5 Getting there. With a bit more map reading and cutlass rattling, you could be a top-notch sky pirate!

6-8 You are a true-blue sky pirate. Join the crew of the Black Sky Wolves immediately!

HAVE YOU READ THE FIRST SWASHBUCKLING SKY PIRATES ADVENTURE?

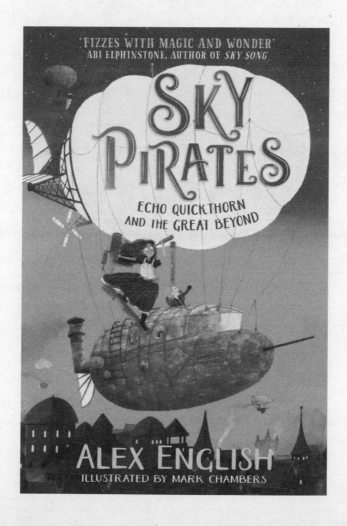

Alex English is a picture book author and a graduate of the Bath Spa University MA Writing for Young People. She currently lives with her family in Reigate.
Sky Pirates: Echo Quickthorn and the Great Beyond was her first middle-grade title and the start of the swashbuckling series.

www.alexenglish.co.uk